The Moonlit Grove

Robin Johnson

Jurasketu Short Fiction

Contact Information: jura.publish@gmail.com

ISBN 978-1-944714-05-5

For Glenden

This story was his idea and wish.

Foreword By The Author

Novella is a favorite format of mine, but it fell out of favor long ago with the demise of literary magazines. The printed book form of a novella was never economically viable to publishers. To make the printed book "thick enough", the publisher had to pad the book with other stories that tended to destroy the unity of the work which makes marketing harder and tends to reduce sales. As a result, publishers either don't publish novellas at all or convince the author to expand the work into a novel length work. I've long thought the rise of e-books would make it popular again. But big, sprawling epics continue to dominate print and e-books and novellas are relatively rare.

This novella was never intended to be marketed in book form and so this version was created to provide hard copies to my friends and specifically my son, Glenden, for whom I wrote the novella based on his wish that his unique idea for a story could be made to exist. To fulfill that wish, I chose the novella form because I needed enough room to explore and develop the idea properly, but I didn't want the idea to become submersed in the more complicated treatment required by a full-blown novel. I wanted to stay focused on the unique idea. And so here we are.

This novella is divided into chapters for both story transition reasons and to provide convenient stopping points for readers who don't have the time to read the entire book in one sitting.

A Note to the Reader

Writers and readers have long struggled to find what actually works best for narrative dialog. In the world of scriptwriting and plays it is very straightforward. The convention is the character name with optional stage direction followed by a colon and then what they say. Simplicity itself. But narrative dialog doesn't follow that convention. And so we have a mish-mash.

I personally have four major complaints about narrative dialog.

First, I hate to spend minutes trying to figure out who said what. I don't know about you, but I get lost very easily when reading dialog. So when the speaker of dialog is not explicitly labeled, I will find myself having to re-read the page to become convinced I know who said what. And often I'm still not sure. For me, that completely destroys the "flow" of the story telling.

He said, "I like chocolate cake."

She said, "Me too."

"Shall we have some?"

"Good idea. When?"

"As soon as we bake another one. The last one is all gone."

"Disappointing."

Second, it is confusing when the speaker is identified "late" in the paragraph of dialog. This is not as bad as the not knowing, but it is irritating when by the natural flow you thought it was one character but then it turns out to be another character. At least you know who was speaking even if belatedly.

Third, I especially find it aggravating when the emotionality of the spoken dialog is conveyed later in the paragraph. It is completely annoying when you read something that sounds mild but turns out was really said angrily. The really great writers let the word choice inform the reader of the emotional state of the speaker – but most writers aren't great.

On the other hand, readers complain that they hate dialog that is snarled, growled, groaned, laughed and smiled. Me too.

Fourth, I also hate pronoun reference errors. Besides, pronouns can be a source of irritation themselves. My given name is ambisexual – and so I've dealt with that a bit.

In my own writing, I rarely or never use the second or third convention where the speaker or emotionality is identified after something is said. But I was willing to risk the first problem of speaker ambiguity. And yet I was troubled by snarled and smiled dialog…

And so I have decided to steal the scriptwriting convention and experimentally adapt for my purposes in this novella.

Speakers are explicitly identified by name - no pronouns except for first person. Emotionality, if required, is specified before the "said". I do use a sprinkling of continued and replied.

Jack smiled and then said, "…"
Jill cringed. She said, "…"
Laughing, Jack said, "…"

Jill continued, "…"
Jack replied, "…"
Jack said, "…"
Jill said, "…"
Pause.
Jill said, "…"

This convention is non-standard in narrative dialog and some readers may be slightly bothered by the repetition in a longer conversation. But since it is rigorously and purposely applied, it seems very comfortable once I became accustomed to the flow.

The Moonlit Grove

Last Night

I stood in the meadow and flapped my arms like a madman. The meadow had no trees. By definition, meadows don't ordinarily have trees. And so this shouldn't have troubled me so much. But last night there were trees. Twelve of them. In a circle...

When I was a youngster, I loved to wander around unsupervised – particularly in the nearby woods. Let us just say my parents were simply permissive rather than irresponsible for not keeping a closer watch on my explorations. Mind you, I was largely careful and never came home seriously injured - just the occasional scrape or wasp sting. So maybe my parents were right.

By the time I was ten, though, I had acquired a taste for nocturnal excursions. Clad in nothing but shorts, I regularly slipped out of the house in the middle of the night to take long moonlit excursions into the woods. I always relished the feel of the pungent, damp night air. I particularly loved the play of the moon shadows. And the feeling of danger in the darkness.

It was a really reckless thing to do – wandering barefoot and barely clothed through the woods in the darkness. But I loved the challenge of navigating my way through prickly forest plants, debris and obstacles. And the feeling of patrolling the woods like a big cat or eluding discovery like a native scout. Admittedly, I stayed to well-worn paths I knew well from daytime exploring, so it was probably not any more reckless than my ordinary reckless behaviors.

I continued making nocturnal hikes as a teenager and on into adulthood. As an adult, I tended to don more suitable attire – like shoes. And while I still loved walking in the moonlight and aromas of the dark, I wasn't quite in love with the feeling of danger anymore. Or the actuality.

The opportunities for nocturnal hiking proved more challenging for the adult me. While North Georgia is replete with wilderness and state parks that allow camping and wandering about in the dark unchallenged, unless I wanted a ghastly daily commute, my career as a banking security analyst limited my ability to live near woods that would be suitable for nocturnal walking about. For some reason, urban and suburban authorities tended to take an unfavorable view of people prowling around private or public woodland during the night. In the end, I chose to live in an overpriced suburban townhome close to work and simply make the long drive out into the countryside to pursue my moonlit hobby when I could manage.

And so this midsummer that happened to overlap the full moon, I had decided to spend a few days at my brother's luxury log cabin in North Georgia near Elijay so I could indulge myself in some extensive nocturnal walking about. The cabin framing was traditional and the furnishings practical, but the bath, kitchen and electrical systems were comfortably modern. More importantly, the cabin property backed up against the Cohutta Wilderness. Like my brother's, most of the cabins in the area were used as base camps for river fishing and hunting, and often doubled as summer getaways.

I had spent a couple of hours that first day, two days ago, a Friday, just exploring the ten acres of cabin property. After I had wolfed down lunch back at the cabin, I had prepared for a longer afternoon hike into the wilderness. Since I never actually camped out, I always used a tactical vest instead of a traditional backpack. I preferred the vest because the weight distribution worked better for me and allowed a more natural and comfortable gait. The downside was the tactical vest and belt didn't provide as much space as a pack. And since I felt that every hike was special, I invariably experimented with what and how much gear and provender to carry. And so I was always randomly stuffing odds and ends that I thought would be useful into the vest and the cargo pockets of the camos I typically wore instead of jeans. A pack would have been better ultimately, but I was stubborn.

I had headed north out into the Cohutta Wilderness and followed a natural trail alongside a creek bed for four kilometers before stumbling upon the wondrous mountain meadow where I now stood. I should have taken advantage of my brother's cabin several years ago, but the opportunities had never worked out right.

The meadow measured about 150 meters across and was punctuated by a granite outcropping in the center. The outcropping consisted of two distinctive stone slabs that rose about a meter above the rest of the meadow and measured meters across. I surmised the soil was likely unusually thin for the area given the lack of trees. Wildflowers grew in sufficient abundance to make the spot meme worthy. The natural path seemed to lead right over to the stones.

The stone slabs were a perfect place to rest and eat something. And so I had taken full advantage. I had decided, without question, that the meadow would be a prime night hike destination. I had trekked carefully back to the cabin and noted landmarks needed for a nocturnal hike. I had even used my favorite backcountry hiking app unimaginatively named Walking Guide to track the excursion. I hadn't planned on using the app during the night hike unless I somehow got lost. I wanted the experience to be relatively old school, but it would be nice to have in an emergency. Even strong and experienced hikers like myself sometimes get lost – especially when we become arrogant and complacent.

Using my tracked hike, I had studied a topographical map and satellite images to make sure I hadn't blithely walked right past a death trap on my initial survey that would swallow me in the middle of the night. Tromping around in the moonlight is only exhilarating if you don't break an important appendage. The satellite images had showed the meadow as long-standing. Topography and images indicated the terrain was relatively gradual except for the creek bed itself. There were no cliffs or obvious sinkholes.

Hiking through wilderness is much safer than driving down the freeway, but evils lurk and can spell discomfort, injury or even death for the unwary, undisciplined or unprepared. Over the years, I've had numerous wilderness encounters. I've stepped over a surprised copperhead. I've stumbled upon a startled black bear. I've gotten lost. I've been attacked and stung on several occasions by yellow jackets, hornets, ants and wasps. I've blundered into poison ivy too many times to count. I worked with a guy who had been infected with Rocky Mountain Spotted Fever and suffered permanent medical issues as a result, and so I diligently check for ticks. And chiggers are simply demon spawn. Like I said, I'm an experienced hiker, and I've learned to make sure I'm always wary, disciplined and prepared.

I had been confident that as long as I kept the creek close to my left on the way out and on my right on the way back, I would be safe. The next morning, I had planned and prepped for a hike to the meadow Saturday night - last night. It was going to be glorious or delicious or awesome or whatever accolade works best for you. It should have been. Except for the circle of trees…

Into the Night

After spending the afternoon slumbering, I woke after dusk and ate a breakfast-dinner of scrambled eggs, bacon and chips. Around 10 pm, I donned my usual tactical vest and gear with the addition of a flashlight, a lightweight walking stick and a snack. I turned off my phone. The phone and flashlight were only for emergencies. I always preferred the night hiking experience of my youth – except for the shoes. I never used the walking stick as a hiking aid, but I have always liked its utility for checking water depth or unstable ground and defense against an unexpectedly aggressive animal.

To my joy, the bright moonlight created shadows, and everything seemed to have a greyish glow. It was too early in the season for cicadas or fireflies, so the woods were relatively quiet and undisturbed. I slowly picked my way along and soaked in the beautiful night. The aromas were earthy and pungent exactly the way I liked. I stopped for several minutes to observe an opossum. Some time later, I spent nearly ten minutes watching two raccoons piddle about the creek catching crayfish.

Around midnight, I saw a patch of moonglow upon the big rocks in the meadow up ahead. I had planned to eat my snack and rest on the rocks. But when I reached the meadow proper, my jaw went slack while my stomach sank. It was the wrong damned meadow.

The meadow was very similar in size and configuration and even included two similarly large rocks now glowing brightly in the moonlight. Yet, instead of just an open field of grass and wildflowers, there was a large circle of twelve dead trees evenly spaced around the stones. The trees were relatively short ranging in height from three to five meters with a sparse set of branches.

Whiskey Tango Foxtrot?

I couldn't believe I had blown the trail. Worse, my satellite pictures had not shown any other meadows near the creek. I must have wandered way off my planned path somehow. *This is going to suck.* I looked back at my path. I could have sworn it looked like what I had memorized from the daylight excursion. But the woods can be very deceptive day or night. I groaned. I still needed to rest, so I decided to see if the stones would be suitable for my break and snack before I attempted to find my way back to the cabin. At least I had the Walking Guide app to avoid getting further lost.

This other meadow did have a similar natural path that led right up to the stones. Oddly, the path seemed to go straight through the nearest dead tree. I scanned the circle. The spacing and orientation seemed to be way too symmetric to have been natural. It seemed likely that someone planted them that way on purpose. They seemed to be all the same species that I couldn't identify in the moonlight. I approached the one astride the path and examined it carefully. The bark was dark brown or black and smooth with occasional ripples. The exposed roots spread evenly almost a meter out from the trunk. The branches spread in a healthy pattern but were devoid of leaves which implied the trees had to have been dead from the previous year. Indeed, I discerned no leaf litter and the grass grew right up to the roots. Oddly, despite being dead, the bark looked alive and felt waxy to the touch.

I shook my head unable to recognize the tree. I decided it was either rare or an exotic imported species. Given that they had most likely been planted deliberately and probably killed by a peculiarity of the local weather, insects or growing conditions, I would have put my bet on an import. The lower branches hung down within reach, so I decided to cut a sample. I pulled a branch down. I was surprised that it exhibited exceptional spring. I let go and watched with fascination as it bounced back and forth before settling down. A dead limb like that should be stiff and much more likely to snap than bounce. I had a weird thought that maybe the trees weren't dead after all but were a peculiar species that didn't leaf out until late summer.

I stood and wondered some more. I nearly pulled out my phone to do a search but decided I might need the phone later to find my way back to the cabin and needed to conserve power. Putting my walking stick down, I pulled the limb down again. Using my left elbow, I held the branch down while I used my left hand to hold a small twig. Then I drew my survival knife with my right. I raised the knife and started to cut a small twig off. Annoyingly, I felt a small drizzle of sap squirt onto the fingers of my knife hand.

Then before I could finish the cut, the branch unexpectedly slipped from under my elbow and snapped up so strongly the knife was knocked from my hands. Fortunately the knife landed harmlessly handle first onto the ground and not blade first into my leg or foot. Somehow, the springing actions caused a second limb to whip around and whack me across the right side of the head knocking me to the ground.

I hurriedly staggered back to my feet and checked for blood with my right hand. I was rewarded with red fingers that seemed to be stinging.

"Damn."

Wiping the blood on my pantleg, I staggered further away from the tree looking for gremlins hiding behind the branches. I was unrewarded. I stood there for a couple minutes trying to recover my composure and decide how badly I was concussed. My right hand throbbed where the limb had thwacked it, but a quick flexing of fingers and hand seemed to conclude it wasn't broken.

"Dammit."

I pulled out my handkerchief, carefully folded it and pressed it against the side of my head to staunch the blood that was running down the side of my face. My skull hurt, and the wound stung, but I hadn't seen stars or other visual anomalies and I didn't feel nauseous. Therefore, I judged I was not actually concussed. No one was around to dispute my opinion, so I decided I could stay in the game.

The head wound stopped bleeding after a few minutes, but my handkerchief was now ruined. I retrieved my walking stick and knife, then staggered over to the stones to rest and apply additional first aid. When I reached the stones, I carefully checked for dangers. The stones seemed devoid of ordinary dangers. But the examination made me rethink my concussion evaluation because the stone slabs looked identical to the stones in the other meadow including a distinctive black vein that jagged its way across the surface of the eastern stone.

I dragged off my tactical vest and sat down. I opened the first aid kit. I used up my sterile pads cleaning the wound. I then used one roll of gauze around my head. I rested and snarfed on the nut and dried fruit mix I had brought for a snack. I sipped some water. Keeping with proper hiker trash protocol, I stuffed the bloody handkerchief and used pads into a bag that I stuffed into the upper cargo pocket on my right pantleg where my snack had been.

While I rested, I observed the weird trees. Based on my observations, I decided that, indeed, I must have a concussion. The branches of the trees were swaying gently in a mild breeze. Except there wasn't a breeze. My head and hand throbbed.

With a sigh of resignation, I pulled out my phone and turned it on. I opened Walking Guide to tell me where I was in relation to my original track. To my dismay, the app appeared to be frozen since it showed I was at the expected terminus in the original meadow. I fiddled with it for a bit trying to get the app to read my correct position. I eventually rebooted the phone, but nothing worked. I checked the compass app for the GPS position, and it showed the same position. I reasoned the phone GPS must be malfunctioning somehow. I gathered my vest and stick, then I walked warily back up the path through the tree circle to the edge of the meadow to see if the GPS showed the positional change.

I was dumbfounded. Walking Guide showed that I was standing on the edge of the meadow exactly where my original track from the daylight reconnoiter hike would have been.

Was I dreaming?

The trees continued to sway in the nonexistent breeze and the bright moonlight.

For later review, I took video and photos of the tree circle.

With a deep breath, I proceeded along the natural path and quickly picked up the creek on my right exactly where it was supposed to be. Anxiously, I marched along keeping the creek in my sights. Remarkably, the GPS and my hiking intuition proved correct when I reached the field that held the cabin. My SUV was parked right where I had left it. I looked back up the hill towards where the meadow would be. The good news was that I was never lost. The bad news was that I was never lost. Dead trees don't grow overnight.

I stumbled into the cabin's combo laundry and mud room and went into post-hike mode. I pulled off the boots and sprayed them with a poison ivy detergent that would also kill any chiggers or ticks. I stripped off my clothing inadvertently pulling loose my head bandage. I threw everything into the laundry and started the cycle. I checked for ticks and found only one hiding on my vest. I put the phone into the charger and went to shower. I paused to examine the head wound in the mirror. It didn't look too bad. It was above the hairline where the scalp heals without too much worry.

I awoke mid-morning. I checked my wound. It looked reasonably fine. I applied a new dressing. My right hand was slightly purple and sore. I rechecked satellite photos and my actual track from Walking Guide. A satellite image from November showed no trees in the meadow. I should have gone home, but I decided I wanted another look at the meadow and the trees.

Two hours later, there I was standing in the meadow waving my arms madly about. The trees were gone. Eventually, I calmed down and scanned for evidence the trees had been there. Somehow, it seemed easier to accept that they had magically appeared and then vanished rather than I had just imagined the whole thing.

I examined the ground carefully where the tree on the path had been. It was clear that something heavy had crushed the meadow flora shaped like the base of a tree. Further examination showed a circular pattern of similar impressions in the grass where the trees had stood last. Then I waved my arms wildly about some more. After a suitable rest, I trudged dejectedly back to the cabin, packed up and went home cutting my vacation short after only three days.

Joanna

My girlfriend, Joanna, and I were well suited for each other. We were both introverted in our own special ways. We both needed a lot of alone time and to the great annoyance of our families had been dating almost ten years without a hint of even living together or much less getting married and having children. She worked as an accountant for the American division of a European multi-national. I worked as a banking analyst monitoring international transactions for money laundering and tax evasion. Our friends assumed it was boring work, but we both liked our jobs. She hadn't expected to hear from me until the following Sunday when I was scheduled to return from my excursion, but she worryingly and readily agreed to come over to my place to see me when I phoned her on the way home.

Joanna wouldn't let me say anything until she had cleaned and dressed my head wound. Then she let me explain how I got injured. I excitedly ran through my experience.

Joanna looked at me funny. She asked, "Did you think to take any pictures?"

My face brightened. I had forgotten I had taken video and photos of the trees.

I said, "I did indeed."

Joanna said, "Show me."

I hooked my phone up to the computer and downloaded the photos and video so I could view them on my ludicrously expensive but beautiful HD gaming monitor. The entire thirty seconds of video was a fascinating scene of grayish snow washing back and forth across black jagged rocks. Or something like that. I sat back stunned in disappointment.

Joanna said, "Are you sure that is the right video?"

I checked the files. There was only one video.

I said, "I never take videos."

Joanna said, "I can see why. Did you have your finger over the lens?"

I shook my head. I said, "I don't know. Let me check the photos."

The two dozen photos were equally disappointing – just grainy blackness.

I slumped in my chair.

Joanna said, "Is your phone camera working properly?"

I said, "Let me see."

A quick video and few photos of Joanna looked perfect.

Joanna said, "Maybe it has trouble in low light?"

I went to the bathroom and took video with the door closed and light off. The results were amazingly good just using the light leaking under the door. I just kept shaking my head in despair. It was similar to that feeling you get when your recording of the big football game is revealed to be a stupid infomercial instead of the game because you selected the wrong channel somehow.

I said, "I guess you're right. I must have been holding a finger or something over the lens in my excitement."

Joanna said, "Garth, how long were you unconscious?"

I said, "I wasn't."

Joanna said, "Are you sure?"

I said, "Oh. Gawd. You don't believe me, do you? Not that I blame you. I don't believe it myself."

Joanna said, "I don't know, Garth. Trees don't just appear and vanish."

I said, "What if they weren't trees? Maybe they were aliens?"

Joanna bobbled her head. She said, "Extraterrestrials masquerading as trees in a remote field? I guess that is more likely than ghosts or something supernatural."

I threw my hands up. I said, "I know, right?"

Joanna said, "Maybe your brother played some elaborate joke on you? It's the kind of thing he would do."

I said, "I called the bastard. He was surprised and vehemently denied doing anything. He seemed genuinely worried that I was hurt. Offered to pick me up."

Joanna sighed. "This is crazy, Garth. I want to see this meadow for myself. Will you take me up there?"

I said, "You don't like hiking."

Joanna said, "Garth. This isn't about hiking. I am worried about you. We need to gather evidence and figure out what really happened."

I said, "But it is a four-kilometer hike into the woods."

Joanna said, "I'm fit. I'll manage. I just don't like bugs."

I said, "Or anything else woodsy."

Joanna said, "Not true. I like trees. Just from a distance."

I said, "Joanna, do you even have clothing and shoes suitable for hiking?"

Joanna frowned. "Well. No. But I can go shopping tomorrow after work."

I said, "Okay."

Joanna said, "It would be nice if you came with me to make sure I got the right stuff."

I said, "Of course."

Joanna said, "I will work tomorrow and then take the rest of the week off so I can focus on this. I am relatively caught up and my boss has been telling me to take a few days off anyway. She thinks I work too much, so she'll be pleased."

I said, "Thank you. I'll refresh our supplies tomorrow. We can drive up Tuesday morning."

Joanna said, "Good. Do you want me to stay with you tonight?"

I said, "No. Not necessary. I know you get up super early for work. I'm good."

Joanna said, "Okay. It's still early. Let us order sushi and watch a movie. That way I can be home by nine."

I leaned over and kissed her. I said, "That would be wonderful."

Powered by Lettuce

One of the things I loved about my townhome was that the master suite was vaulted with curtainless high windows facing South. Sunlight and moonlight could stream unimpeded into the room. I had acquired various pieces of art glass that gleamed in the natural lighting giving the room a dreamlike quality. Unfortunately, Joanna hated the unrelenting sparkle of shadows and rainbows. That meant when we did spend the night together, it was invariably at her house which was exceptionally nice but very conventional.

I woke in the middle of the night from a strange dream with the strong moonlight playing across the room in a dazzle of interesting shadows. In the dream, I needed batteries and so I went to an unbranded warehouse store. The floors were finished concrete with that distinctive musty cement smell. The aisles were unusually spacious, and the store was relatively quiet. After wandering around a bit, I spotted what I thought were large, white batteries racked at the end of an aisle. When I got to the rack, I realized they were actually small fire extinguishers. But they were not ordinary fire extinguishers. They were special "green" fire extinguishers made from vegetable matter. And green italic lettering on the bottles proudly proclaimed, *"POWERED BY LETTUCE"*.

I took the opportunity to get up and relieve my bladder. Instead of immediately returning to bed, I stood with my back to the windows and admired the play of lights. After a brief while, I felt a sudden burning sensation and discomfort in my lower back. I tried to stretch it out by touching my toes. Unexpectedly, a horrible wave of nausea washed over me that dropped me to my knees. I staggered back up to my feet just in time for my entire body to become painfully rigid. I couldn't move. Then I stopped breathing. Everything went completely silent and black.

I'm dying.

I was floating. *Or not.* I was still conscious. *Or not.* Somehow, I seemed to be touching the floor, the walls and the vaulted ceiling. My mind swirled with murky sensations from every direction. I seemed to be *feeling* everything around me – near and far. I didn't seem to be me. I seemed larger and spread apart. *Or not.*

I am definitely dying.

I still felt completely rigid. I couldn't breathe or engage any muscles or anything. I seemed to be puddled on the floor but touching the ceiling and walls here and there. Through the fog of sensations emerged stronger areas that seemed to be wires… and pipes… and nails… and screws… and light fixtures… and my clock… and my phone… and the sink… and the kitchen appliances… and my little pot of cacti… It was like seeing by feeling. My mind seemed to be creating weird imagery of false color showing everything in my townhome and beyond. *Or not.*

After a time, the fog cleared, and I was overwhelmed with three-dimensional false color imagery that extended in all directions. I tried to focus on something nearby. I reeled as the entirety of my bed jumped into focus. I could see the structure of inner foam core and wooden frame as clearly as the covers and pillow. Everything swirled as my mind attempted to assign colors to the sensations.

How could I be dying if I can still think clearly?

I must still be in a dream state.

I could never recall having a dream where I couldn't actually do anything other than receive sensations that resembled a CAT scan of the entire world. This was crazy. I flailed my arms in despair. *Or not. Wait. Something moved.*

I tried to move my arms again. The sensation of touching the walls seemed to oscillate back and forth. The imagery had shimmered slightly in a disconcerting way. I tried to move my arms again. It had the same effect except now I felt woozy and foggy. I decided against further attempts. Eventually I recovered, and the fog lifted.

This is one damned strange dream.

Sometimes, I'll find that a dream will feed into a partial waked state and becomes essentially editable. Both bad dreams and ordinary dreams can then be worked into a narrative that I would consciously prefer. It seems like cheating to fix a nightmare, but it was satisfying nonetheless. I decided to alter this dream since I was likely in a partially waked state given my level of self-awareness.

No matter what I tried, I couldn't shut down the imagery or change it. The false color sensations refused to change upon application of my will. I could seemingly narrow my focus and the fine details would seem clearer. If I changed the focus and returned, the fine details remained the same.

Fuck. I must be dead, and I was wrong about the afterlife.

I'm now a ghost or something horrible.

I wondered if I could perceive other ghosts or whatever I now was. I cast my focus further afield. I quickly located people, but they were clearly just my living and breathing neighbors. I willfully calmed the rising panic in my mind and resolved to just wait for the nightmare to pass. I focused on my clock to see if time was passing, but the digital display eluded my ability to focus.

Time passed… *Or not.* And then some more time. Various nocturnal animals flitted in the distance almost imperceptible in the continuing flood of psychedelic sensations. More time… Then a stirring next door. My neighbors, a very friendly young couple, had awakened and moved about their bedroom. Then they returned to bed and apparently began making love. I tried desperately to avert my attention, but with almost nothing else to command my focus, I realized it was impossible to not observe them in bizarre x-ray detail. While I was not exactly new to observing sex acts, in those other cases, the participants had knowingly shared a record of the event. I decided to pretend it wasn't happening. I was probably dead anyway and shouldn't suffer from embarrassment. *Or not.*

Eventually the couple completed their morning activities and left for work. I knew they usually left right around dawn in the midsummer. That had to mean time had really passed and this nightmare would end. Suddenly, everything fuzzed and snapped to black.

I found myself kneeling on my shins, face on the floor and arms splayed out. I sat up and immediately felt sick. I wretched violently and vomited bile onto the laminate floor. I sucked in several hard breaths and collapsed sideways overcome with vertigo. Having learned a usually effective treatment for severe vertigo several years before, I turned the side of my head to the floor for several seconds and then turned the other way to restore my equilibrium.

"Fuck."

I struggled to my feet and casually looked around as the light from the rising sun flooded the room. I noticed what looked like dust and broken glass scattered around.

Omigawd.

I put my hand over my mouth and stared wide-eyed for an eternity.

The walls and ceiling looked like they had been gnawed on. The window frames had been marred and several of the curtain rods had been dislodged. To my dismay, the flooring near where I had vomited showed numerous deep scratches that radiated outward in an asymmetric pattern from almost certainly the spot where I had woken from the nightmare. I croaked in despair when I saw that most of my expensive art glass had been smashed into a spray of small pieces and dust.

Glass. Broken. Dust.

Standing naked and most importantly barefoot in a room full of broken glass mixed with drywall dust wasn't exactly my most comfortable moment. After a quick scan, I was relieved to find I wasn't bleeding. Luckily, the area where I had lain was relatively clean of the debris. I looked to the door and the kitchen where I kept the vacuum, a broom and most importantly my shoes. Unfortunately, a zillion pieces of blue glass from a once beautiful blue wave glass sculpture had splashed in front of the door and down the hall.

What the hell had I done?

I decided that figuring how to get to my shoes took priority over anything else at that moment given that walking barefoot through broken glass seemed like a bad plan. I looked around for an improvisational inspiration. After a few moments, I came up with a plan. Without moving my feet, I leaned forward and carefully pulled the summer-weight duvet off the bed and lowered it slowly top down onto the floor. I gently stepped onto the duvet. Without picking up my feet, I slid and skated the duvet forward towards the door and down the hall. It took me nearly an hour to vacuum and wipe up the glass and dust. And I would need a new duvet in addition to extensive drywall repairs.

Doctor J

I sat sipping coffee at the kitchen table bemoaning my destroyed art glass collection and wondering why and what I had used to wreck my bedroom in some bizarre sleep walking episode that must have overlapped my psychedelic dream sequence. The doors and windows were still locked and bolted. My alarm system had not gone off. I was the only person in the house. *Or was I?* I wasted twenty minutes poking into every possible hiding place with my walking stick.

The stick?

A careful examination showed not a hint of drywall dust and I could see trail dirt from the hike yesterday-night, so I hadn't cleaned it to remove the evidence. I spent another ten minutes fruitlessly looking for some other items that held evidence of drywall dust that could have been used and returned to their place.

After due consideration, I decided that in my sleep walking episode I must have destroyed my art glass collection by throwing the pieces at the walls. I told myself that head injuries and stress can produce strange sleep behaviors. The correct action at this point was to text my doctor. Uncharacteristically, I did. She told me to come over immediately to her office. I was sitting in an exam room by 9:15 AM trying not to be worried sick that I was sick.

Her real name was Juliana Galway, but everyone called her Doctor J. She had acquired the nickname as a star forward for the University of Georgia basketball team where she was known for her exceptional ballhandling skills and plans to attend medical school. Unsurprisingly, she specialized in sports, performance and metabolic medicine while also running a general practice.

Doctor J waved off the nurse who was trying to take my vitals.

I was seated on the exam table looking disheveled and very concerned – because I was both.

Doctor J eyed me carefully before folding her long brown arms across her chest and asking, "Okay. What exactly is going on? Every detail."

I said, "Saturday night, I was taking a nocturnal hike from my brother's cabin up in Elijay. And I came across some strange trees. I was pulling on a branch to cut a twig sample when I lost my grip resulting in a bashed hand and a whack to the side of the head."

I showed her my bruised hand and pointed to the side of my head. I hadn't redressed the wound that morning since it wasn't bleeding. My hand and head seemed to be healing very quickly.

Doctor J gave me a quizzical look. "Nocturnal?"

I said, "Yeah. At night."

Doctor J looked at me with that patented physician look of incredulity. "Isn't that stupid and dangerous?"

I said, "I'm careful and experienced. And the experience is usually worth the marginal risks. It is a regular habit of mine."

Doctor J nodded in a resigned fashion and asked, "Did you lose consciousness?"

I said, "No."

Doctor J said, "Nausea? Headaches?"

I said, "No concussion symptoms until last night."

Doctor J gave me a quizzical look.

I said, "I was having a strange nightmare and apparently sleepwalking. When I woke from the nightmare, I found myself out of bed on the floor retching. I had wrecked my bedroom, breaking my art glass and damaging the walls. After that, I decided I should be checked by a professional."

Doctor J nodded. "The last bit is logical. Let me see the hand."

I extended the hand where she gave it a cursory look and had me do various things to prove it wasn't broken. She then looked at my scalp and muttered.

Doctor J said, "Look at me. Follow my finger."

I followed.

Doctor J said, "Good."

Then she blinded me with her mini flashlight.

Doctor J said, "Eyes are good."

Next, she used an otoscope to look in my ears and up my nose. I tried not to squirm away.

Doctor J said, "No evidence of bleeding."

I helpfully added, "That is good."

Then she checked my reflexes. She deemed I

was sufficiently reflexive.

Doctor J did not seem relieved. "Everything looks observably normal. But post-head injury nausea is not something we like to see."

I said, "I know. That is why I'm here."

Doctor J said, "Do you feel dizzy or nauseous right now?"

I shrugged and said, "No. Other than a little itchy, I feel perfectly fine."

Doctor J stood back and said, "Well. The weird sleep and nausea symptoms indicate a CT scan and some blood work."

Doctor J tapped on the computer a bit and hemmed. Then she said, "Good news. There is an opening at ten-thirty with the radiology group down the hall. After the CT scan, I want you to come back after the scan and sit in the waiting room until the radiologist and I can review the results. The nurse will draw blood shortly."

Unhappily I said, "Okay. Other than a concussion – what are the other causes of nausea?"

Doctor J shrugged. She said, "Toxins, drugs and infections."

I said, "That seems like a narrow list."

Doctor J chuckled.

I said, "Can you tell which one using a blood test?"

Doctor J said, "Maybe. The blood tests I've ordered include a full liver panel and blood counts. Abnormal results can indicate poisoning or infection. Based on the results, the lab pathologist will order further tests for the most likely toxins, drugs or infections so indicated."

I said, "And if the bloodwork is normal?"

Doctor J said, "Medicine is replete with mysteries mundane and exotic."

Doctor J quirked an eyebrow and asked, "Did you eat anything from the woods?"

I said, "I just go trekking around. I am not a survivalist or gourmet. I only ate and drank stuff I brought with me."

Doctor J said, "That would seemingly rule out poisonous mushrooms or plants. Vertigo is a common symptom of mushroom poisoning."

I said, "No mushrooms - wild or store bought."

Doctor J said, "Good."

By 11:45, I was sitting in Doctor J's office.

Doctor J said, "The CT was normal. No internal bleeding. No visible skull injury."

I said, "That would be good."

Doctor J nodded and said, "Yes. The bloodwork won't be completed for many hours. I will call you once I get the results. I suspect the nausea was just a combination of disturbed sleep cycle and stress caused by your nighttime misadventure and maybe lingering effects of the head injury."

I nodded sheepishly.

Doctor J continued, "For the next few weeks, you need to be careful and avoid activities that might cause another concussion. Overlapping concussions are particularly serious. If you experience more nausea or new symptoms, don't hesitate to contact me. And I want you to come back to see me once I have the bloodwork."

Back home by 12:30 PM, I texted Joanna, "I was nauseous last night. So I went to see Dr J. I feel fine now and back home. Physical exam was normal. CT head scan showed nothing - I am brainless. Will have to wait a few days on bloodwork. I am supposed to be careful in case it was a mild concussion."

A few minutes later, Joanna texted back, "Yikes. Not good."

I texted, "Yeah."

I should have just called but instead I spent a minute creating a text that said, "Hey. I need to have my bedroom repainted. I accidentally damaged the drywall the other day. It needs repair. I've been thinking about a color change anyway. But I'll need to stay at your place for a couple of days sometime next week most likely. Okay?"

Joanna texted a "sure" and several hearts.

I texted a smile.

Joanna texted, "Leaving work at 3. Meet me at my house at 3:30?"

I texted, "k". Then I added several kiss emojis.

Joanna texted a heart back.

I poked around on the Internet for a while to distract myself before heading over to Joanna's place. The Monday outrage level seemed to be below normal, but I found some articles about cryptography that proved interesting.

I arrived just before Joanna, and after a brief kiss we went inside. Her house, lawn and gardens had been lifted straight out of a home magazine with everything always in immaculate condition. She always took no credit for it though and made it known that she had hired everything out from design to maintenance. She claimed she loved nice stuff but didn't have the time, skills or talent for that kind of work. She liked to say she was converting her financial skills and talent into quality of life. And with a hint of amusement, readily admitted that she had asked her designers to be boringly conventional and functional. While boring and conventional, it is hard to argue with really nice especially when any inconvenient maintenance is handled by someone else.

Inside, Joanna looked me over carefully. She said, "You look well enough. How do you feel?"

I said truthfully, "I feel perfectly fine if a little stressed about trees and an undetermined medical problem."

Joanna said, "The trees. I have a terrible feeling the not-really-there trees and the nausea are related somehow."

I said, "Maybe. You still don't believe me, do you?"

Joanna replied, "Yes and no. The story is not believable. But I believe in you. I get paid gobs of money to discover what is wrong when the numbers don't add up. Your story doesn't add up – so we have to investigate and determine what and why. Until I see this meadow up close and get a feel for what is going on, I want to keep my thoughts to myself."

I slumped a little and said, "I understand. It

seems like madness."

Joanna shook her head. She said, "Not madness. Just weirdness. We'll figure it out."

I nodded with resignation hoping she was right.

Joanna raised an eyebrow. She said, "Did Doctor J say you could still have sex?"

I said, "She said to be careful and avoid another concussion. I've never suffered a concussion having sex before. So as long as we don't try something unconventional and dangerous, I think it would be okay."

Joanna said, "Well?"

I said, "I guess I'm ready to go shopping."

Joanna bowed her head. She said, "I was offering to try and cheer you up with some lovemaking."

I said, "Oh. Yes. I think that might help. Sorry."

Joanna said, "Don't be sorry. Come over here and kiss me."

I needed no further coaching…

Some time later, I got up from the bed to go pee. As I walked to the bathroom, I heard a gasp.

I stopped and looked back. I said, "Are you okay?"

Joanna said, "When did you get a tattoo?"

I said, "What? I don't have a tattoo?"

Joanna said, "Then what is that on your back?"

Joanna jumped up from the bed, came over and grabbed my shoulder. I struggled slightly wanting to maneuver in front of the large framed mirror by the closet. She rubbed it, but then let me look in the mirror.

What the fuck…

An incredibly intricate and complex pattern of leaves and branches in green, yellow, red and black woven into a sprawling spiral covered a portion of my lower left back. Within the pattern, the larger elements were composed of equally intricate smaller patterns that could have existed on their own. My first thoughts were that the design was stunningly beautiful and belonged on a much better canvas than my blotchy skin. Next, I rubbed the design and felt nothing but ordinary skin.

Joanna peered closer and proclaimed, "It seems embedded under the skin like a tattoo."

I said, "Like a tattoo? Isn't that the definition? Do you think it's permanent?"

Joanna said, "Depends on the ink that was used I would guess."

I said, "Yeah. But how did it get there? It's not like you can get a tattoo unknowingly. Especially an intricate one that would take many hours to complete. I know I didn't have a tattoo when I returned from the hike in the woods because I checked for ticks in the mirror. I would have noticed the tattoo."

Joanna said, "Maybe a bored master decided to drug you and spend hours tattooing a masterpiece on your back?"

I nodded. "That would explain the horrible nightmare and nausea I had last night. It seemed like one of those psychedelic trips they always show in the movies."

Joanna said, "I was joking."

I said, "Sometimes art imitates life. Sometimes life imitates art. Sometimes life is a joke. Sometimes the joke is life."

I shook my head. I said, "Joanna – what the fuck is happening to me?"

Joanna hugged me and said, "It's going to be alright. We'll figure it out."

I said, "And what if we can't?"

Joanna shrugged and said, "Life can suck sometimes."

I said, "Great."

I said, "Should I show this to Doctor J?"

Joanna said, "Not yet. She would think you're crazy. I still want to look at that meadow. Let's get dressed and go shopping."

Three hours later, we returned having successfully obtained hiking boots, khakis, socks and a lightweight hiking jacket that met my stringent performance specifications and Joanna's significantly less stringent style requirements. We packed, watched a movie and tucked in early.

The Neighbor

The bees and butterflies flitted in the sunlit-warmed meadow when we exited the substantially cooler woods onto the path. The stones and path were unchanged. There were no trees in the meadow.

I said, "This is the meadow and path. Up here."

I moved up the path and quickly found the spot where the tree had squatted on the path. The impression had only faded slightly. The flowers and grass had been crushed and the ground indented a couple of centimeters that clearly matched what the base of a tree would form.

I pointed. "There. See it?"

Joanna, hands on hips, scanned the impression and then looked about the meadow.

She said, "Wow. That is crazy. There are others?"

I said, "Yes. I'll show you."

We took more time than I did last time surveying the other impressions. We counted a total of twelve which matched my memory of the number of trees.

Joanna looked at me and said, "Is there a way to tell if anyone or anything else walked up to or away from these spots?"

I shrugged and said, "I'm sure an experienced

tracker could tell something like that. I have limited skill in that area. I guess we could try looking around."

She frowned and said, "I guess so. It wouldn't hurt to try. We should have recruited someone to help us."

I said, "On short notice, I'm sure we could have found someone willing to help us track down some walking trees."

Joanna said, "Probably not. Just look anyway."

We poked around pretending to be trackers and not unsurprisingly found nothing of interest. I took several minutes of video at close range around the impressions in some vague hope of crowdsourcing or finding an expert that could magically discern something from a video.

Eventually, Joanna gave up and we started back. At the edge of the meadow, I noticed that the natural creek path forked northwards a few meters inside the woods. I pointed that out to Joanna, and we explored a couple hundred meters until we saw it diverged to the northwest away from the meadow. It wasn't a marked trail in Walking Guide, but we looked carefully for prints and spotted some definite deer prints and what we thought were a few human shoe prints. Maybe.

I said, "It is probably just an animal path and maybe a stray hiker."

Joanna said, "Well. At least it is possible someone was up here."

I said, "I dunno. Let's head back and think."

Joanna said, "Yes. I think we should come back at night. If the trees are ghosts or some other trick of the night, they aren't going to be visible in daylight."

I said, "Ghosts? Trick of the night?"

Joanna said, "You got anything better?"

I said, "No. But…"

Joanna said, "But what?"

I said, "I'm not exactly a believer in the supernatural, but what if the place really is cursed or something? You might be in danger. It's bad enough that I'm cursed or whatever."

Joanna considered a moment. She said, "I'll take my chances. I need to know."

I said, "Let's talk when we get back and can think some more."

We returned to the cabin where I guided Joanna through the post-hiking rituals. We quickly showered and changed into something comfortable. I convinced her to sit outside with a beer to discuss our plans for a nighttime hike. I wasn't entirely comfortable leading Joanna on a nocturnal excursion through the woods. But maybe some trick of the moonlight would expose itself and we would have an explanation. I spent over an hour drilling Joanna in the details of tromping through the woods at night. Fortunately, she was reasonably athletic, agile, fit and not particularly clumsy even if she didn't like the woods, particularly the bugs. And this wasn't a pleasure hike, so I would be fully utilizing the available technology.

We were about to go back inside when I noticed a woman walking purposefully down the road, cross onto the cabin property, and approach us. She waved from a distance to indicate she walked to talk. We got up to greet her.

I said, "Good afternoon. Can we help you?"

She said, "Hi. I'm your neighbor up the road a ways. My name is Bonnie Otter. I thought Joe had a new car and a new girlfriend and so I thought I would stop by and say hello. Obviously, you aren't Joe but are you related to Joe? You look very similar."

Bonnie was wearing an ordinary blue polo, jeans and a pair of elaborately decorated over-the-calf moccasins. Her long, black hair was pulled back in a ponytail. Lines around her dark brown eyes suggested she was older, but otherwise she had a very youthful appearance.

I smiled and said, "Not surprising since I'm Joe's younger brother, Garth."

I pointed to Joanna and said, "This is my girlfriend Joanna Kensington."

Joanna nodded and said, "Pleased to meet you."

Bonnie nodded in return and said, "Likewise. I apologize for disturbing you. Joe and I are good friends. I'll be on my way."

Bonnie started to turn away.

I said, "No, sit. Don't be ridiculous. You aren't disturbing us. Any friend of Joe's is certainly a friend of mine."

I looked at Joanna who nodded helpfully.

I said, “The weather is so nice. We’d love to sit out here and chat for a spell. Would you like something to drink or eat? We have beer and spring water.”

Joanna said, “I can make some tea.”

Bonnie said, “No thank you, I’m fine.”

I said, “Do you come up here often?”

Bonnie smiled and said, “I live here year-round.”

I said, “Awesome. How long?”

Bonnie said, “All my life.”

Joanna said, “I hope you don’t mind me asking, are you Cherokee?”

Bonnie waggled her head. She said, “I’m not Cherokee. I’m Muscogee.”

Joanna said, “Wow. Cool. I love the moccasins. Are they traditional?”

Bonnie looked down at her legs and said, “Goodness no. They are traditional only in the abstract sense. While I use only natural methods in the tanning process of the deerskin, I use a fancy sewing machine and modern shoe techniques to make them. The decorative elements are simply personal expression. I consider them practical artwork.”

Thinking of gift potential, I said, “Does that mean you make them for sale?”

Bonnie nodded. She said, “I make about forty custom pairs a year as a hobby both as gifts and some for sale.”

Joanna talked over me and asked, “How much for a pair?”

Bonnie smiled. She said, "Each pair is unique, and custom fitted to the purchaser."

I said, "Of course. Expensive. How much?"

Bonnie said, "Ordinarily, I charge twenty-five hundred dollars a pair, all in advance, with delivery in six to nine months. And I only sell to people that I believe will actually wear them and deserve them. But I only take about fifteen to twenty orders a year. Instead, I prefer to make them as gifts of love to folks that are nominated by the Otter Clan. Everyone says they are a coveted gift. I will take their word for it. I put considerable love and effort into them. I always hope they are well received and worn. They are intended to be practical."

Joanna said, "Oh, wow. In that case, I do not feel worthy to accept responsibility for owning a pair even if you thought me worthy should I be brave enough to ask."

Bonnie said, "That is extremely kind of you. But they are merely things. I just hate putting effort into something for folks that covet things but don't appreciate them the same way I do. I know that sounds crazy and contradictory."

Joanna laughed. She said, "Exactly. You're an artist. I'm afraid you would deem me a mere dilettante once you got to know me."

Bonnie smiled. She said, "I appreciate your honesty. A character trait that I believe overshadows minor character flaws. Tell me more about yourself."

Joanna surprised me by actually talking

about herself for a good long while before she reverted to her ordinary reticence. I took up the slack and managed to give a good accounting of myself. Bonnie had kept us going with insightful questions and enthusiasm.

I've always found the human ability to conduct ordinary social conversation when under serious duress as rather remarkable. In fact, it is generally considered improper to burden a stranger with your own troubles, no matter how dire or immediate, unless you would be willing and able to provide help without reservation should the situation be reversed.

Finally, I realized I should ask her something.

I said, "Bonnie. I need to ask you a strange question about the area since you have lived here a long time. Can you promise to answer honestly?"

Bonnie gave me a long, strange look and said, "Okay. I will try."

I nodded towards the creek and said, "Are you familiar with the meadow with the two large flat rocks about three miles to the north on the eastern side of the creek?"

Bonnie shrugged and said, "I think I know the one. It is a nice spot. I often hike up there in the fall and spring."

I said, "Has anyone ever reported anything strange happening there?"

Bonnie raised an eyebrow. With a laugh, she said, "A strange happening? Like what? The folks up here are an eclectic mix but overall level-headed, practical and conservative. We live up here to avoid the excitement of the modern world. A strange happening here might be considered commonplace in the big city, if you know what I mean."

I frowned. I decided to change tactics.

I said, "Have you ever been up there at night?"

Bonnie muffled a sharp intake of breath and then shrugged broadly. She said, "Folks don't bother to go camping much around here since we already live in the woods. And we don't typically need to go that far back into the woods during hunting season to reach quota. We only grant access to bow hunters across our property along this stretch. We like things quiet up here. I only bow hunt myself."

I nodded realizing that seemed to make sense. Joe was an avid bow hunter and only used firearms for bird hunting. I sighed heavily.

Bonnie gave me a concerned look. She asked, "Are you okay?"

I said, "Mostly."

Joanna said, "He saw some ghosts up there the other night."

Bonnie said, "Night?"

I said, "Yes. I took a nocturnal hike to the meadow. I bumped my head on a ghost."

I tilted my head and pointed to the head wound that was not unexpectedly healing well.

Bonnie gave me a strange look. She said, "A ghost? The moon casts weird shadows sometimes. Trees can leap out of the dark in your way if you're not careful. If you know what I mean."

Joanna and I exchanged glances.

I said, "Indeed they can. But it wasn't exactly like that. I was definitely in the meadow away from the trees."

Bonnie furrowed her brow and said, "I see. When?"

I said, "Saturday night, on the Full Moon."

Bonnie breathed deeply and said, "Odd."

With a sigh, I said, "I know you don't believe me. I must sound crazy."

Bonnie said, "Yes. But I know that feeling myself sometimes."

There was a long pause.

Bonnie said, "Other than the bump on the head, are you okay?"

Joanna said, "No," and I said, "Yes," at the same time.

Bonnie raised both eyebrows. I glanced at Joanna.

I said with a smile, "I'm fine. No lingering effects. Joanna thinks I'm crazy for claiming it was a ghost."

Joanna shrugged.

Bonnie said, "Do not worry. I don't judge others in regard to such things. I've lived too many years to be certain what is real and what is imagined and even if there is a difference."

Bonnie looked up the at the sky and stood up. She said, "I've wasted too much of your afternoon already. I should be on my way."

Joanna and I nodded with understanding.

Bonnie started to walk away and then stopped.

She turned back slightly and said, "You know, I'm a very experienced tracker. Too late today, but if you want, I would be happy to walk up there with you tomorrow to take a look and see what I can discover. I could at least rule out some things for you."

I glanced at Joanna. She shrugged.

I said, "Actually. That would be helpful. What time?"

Bonnie said, "Nine? I meet you here?"

I said, "Okay. Sure. We'll be up by eight for certain. You can join us for coffee if you like."

Bonnie said, "Very good. That sounds nice. Tomorrow then."

Joanna and I watched Bonnie walk back to the road and out of sight with a final wave.

Joanna said, "Well. I guess we could have gotten an experienced tracker on short notice if we had known eh?"

I said, "I suppose. She sure seems friendly enough. Should we trust her?"

Joanna said, "What do you mean? She was pretty understanding despite your crazy talk."

I said, "Exactly. Doesn't that make you nervous?"

Joanna said, "Call your brother and see if her story checks out?"

I said, "Good idea."

My brother quickly confirmed that Bonnie was indeed his not-too-close friend, but claimed she was incredibly kind and quick to provide help if she could. I decided my need was greater than my instinctive lack of trust.

Joanna said, "Should we cancel our nocturnal hike until Bonnie can look the meadow over with us tomorrow?"

I mulled that over and said, "No. I think we should go as planned."

Joanna said, "Good."

Moon Glow

We took a four-hour nap and headed out by 7:30 PM. Sunset would be near 9 PM, so we would have plenty of time before sunset to reach the meadow without having to walk in the dark. I wanted to wait in the woods near the meadow until well after dark to see what might appear before we entered the meadow ourselves. The disadvantage with this plan was that the moonrise was not until just after midnight and so we would be sitting in the dark for several hours.

The way was now very familiar to me and so we made excellent time reaching the meadow fifteen minutes before sunset. I found what I thought was a decent observation post behind some mountain laurel and dogwoods that appeared to be free of dangerous or noisome critters. We sat down to wait and watch in the twilight. We would have about two hours of total darkness before moonrise. While we waited, owls hooted in the distance. A slight breeze rustled the leaves now and again, but otherwise the forest was pleasantly quiet.

At the expected moon rise, we remained silent and still. I trembled slightly with anticipation. The moon was still nearly full and bathed the meadow in bright, silvery light. But nothing appeared. And nothing moved. We kept waiting for almost an hour.

I said, "Well. Nothing so far."

Joanna said, "No. Shall we enter to see if something triggers?"

I said, "I guess. I'm not sure. I encountered the trees around eleven-thirty, and it's already past twelve-thirty."

Joanna said, "Might as well try."

I stood up, looked back over my shoulder and said, "Okay. Be careful. Don't trip on a root."

And then, naturally, I took one step, caught a root and face planted.

I groaned and cursed softly. I said reflexively, "I'm okay."

In reality, my right side was wailing where I had clipped a rock. I struggled to my knees and stood up. And groaned.

Joanna stifled a guffaw.

I laughed painfully too. I said, "I'm not normally this clumsy."

My tactical vest, belt, jacket and black dri-fit undershirt were all askew. I decided my wailing side needed a looksee. I unbuckled my belt and pulled off my vest.

I said, "I need to check my side."

I unbuttoned my jacket and pulled up the black dri-fit shirt I was wearing. A brief inspection revealed no blood and so I tucked the shirt back into my trousers. I stood for a moment, arms akimbo and surveyed the scene in the moonlight.

Joanna said, "Hey. I would swear your tattoo glowed in the moonlight."

I said, "Hun? Do you mean reflected?"

Joanna said, "No. It was glowing."

I said, "Trick of the light."

I gathered up the vest and walked into the meadow using the pathway. Joanna followed. I marched out and placed the vest on the nearest slab.

Joanna said, "Seriously. It was glowing. Can you pull your shirt up so I can get another look?"

I said, "Okay. Fine."

Annoyed, I shimmied off my jacket and then I pulled the shirt completely off.

I said, "There."

Joanna said, "Turn your back to the moonlight so I can get a good look."

I took a couple of steps away from the rock and turned. I posed with upraised arms. I said, "Well?"

Joanna gasped. She said, "That is really weird."

Suddenly, I felt a slight burning sensation and a sudden wave of nausea. I stiffened. Everything went black.

Moon fucking hell. It's happening again.

Just like before my perception became psychedelic. I could perceive Joanna stumbling backwards. The woods and meadow teemed with sensations near and far. I tried to wave my arms. Everything shimmered – but unlike last time – I didn't feel dizzy. *Or not.*

I scanned about the meadow but perceived nothing unexpected for a meadow and woods. The granite slabs seemed black and indistinct. I thought back and remembered rocks and ground being the same in the previous dream.

I focused on Joanna. She had backed ten meters away with the slabs between us. She was standing, facing my direction with fists clenched at her sides.

Joanna!

She did not stir.

Fuck.

I tried frantically waving my arms again. This time I felt dizzy.

She's moving.

Joanna circled to her right. She came closer but then walked a complete circle around me. She stood arms akimbo for a long time. She circled back to her left and then spent several minutes scanning the meadow. Eventually, she squatted down with her arms dangled across her knees. She stayed that way for a long time…

What the fuck is she doing?

I focused on her and could perceive her heart beating and lungs inhaling/exhaling. She seemed remarkably calm. Eventually, she got up slowly and cautiously approached me. She raised a hand and then touched me. I could feel her hand, but I couldn't determine where. Then she seemed to be rubbing both hands on me. *Or not.*

Could I perceive myself?

I tried to focus my perception on myself to find where she was touching. I couldn't make any sense of the imagery. I could sense her hands, but everything was fuzzy that corresponded to me. I redoubled my focus on Joanna. But this seemed to make things worse. In addition to seeing inside her, it seemed like I was seeing her from all directions at once. *Or not.* I concentrated on reconciling the imagery but that overwhelmed me causing everything to blur into a spray of swirling colors.

Defeated, I tried to relax and just let my perception float. The blurring lessened and Joanna came back into focus. She tapped her fist on me.

That felt weird.

Joanna squatted down and examined the ground. She grabbed my foot. *Or not.* Then she grabbed another foot. And then a third foot. *Third?* I continued to float and decided that I had what seemed like six or seven feet touching the grass.

Joanna got back up and walked back to the slab, climbed up and sat down with her arms wrapped around her knees. And she remained that way for a long time…

Eventually, she turned to her side. I surmised she went to sleep.

I scanned into the woods. Several deer nosed about one end of the meadow for awhile. I followed a copperhead as it tracked down and ate an unsuspecting field rat. Several opossums wandered here and there. An owl swooped by and gathered up a baby rabbit. The circle of life played out in psychedelic colors.

My thoughts drifted to what had happened

to me. I tried to focus on the sky. Oddly, it was empty – just blackness. I couldn't perceive stars or the moon. I peered into the ground. I thought I could indistinctly sense roots, rocks, worms, burrows, rodents and whatnot, but not very deep. The slabs seemed very opaque and quiet. I concluded my dream sense must be limited by distance and didn't extend far into dense objects. *Or not.*

Joanna continued to sleep while I dreamt or whatever it was.

I decided to float until sunrise…

Joanna stirred some time later and sat back up. She looked around. She got down from the slab and cautiously moved away from the slabs.

Where is she going now?

I brought my focus to see what she was doing and realized too late she was just taking a pee. She returned and drank from her water bottle. She stood and stared at me for a long while. Then she scanned the sky. Shaking her head, she climbed back on the slab and sat cross-legged with chin propped in hand.

Just float until sunrise and the dream will end. Just float…

I checked on Joanna periodically, but other than shifting position a few times she just sat there – watching me, I think.

Without warning, everything fuzzed and then went black. When my vision returned, I found myself retching on my hands and knees. There was a hand on my bare shoulder.

A voice likely attached to the hand said, "It's going to be okay."

That is what they always tell the dying.

I shivered from the heaving, but then I was able to catch my breath and calm my body. I sat back on my haunches and let my arms dangle. The hand moved to the top of my shoulder. I glanced up to make sure it was indeed Joanna. It was.

Joanna said, "You're gonna to be okay."

I said, "That seems unlikely."

She sighed.

I said, "Okay. What happened to me?"

Joanna said, "You morphed into a tree."

I said, "I fucking what?"

Joanna said, "You went stiff, your clothes disintegrated in a cloud of dust, and your skin turned dark, mottled gray. Then your legs, body and head slowly melted into a tree trunk thing. Surface roots grew out from your feet. Next, your arms melted into larger limbs with numerous small branches. Then several branches burst forth from your top and spread out several meters. There were no leaves, though."

I said, "That is fucking impossible."

That is what I said, but I knew she was telling the truth. I could even see root impressions all around me. And my pants and shoes were missing.

Joanna said, "Obviously not."

I said, "When I was a kid, I often dreamed of being a superhero. Shapeshifting into a tree seems like a damned useless superpower."

Joanna said, "Seems more like a nominally benign werewolf curse. It happened the moment you exposed your tattoo to the moonlight."

I said, "Omigawd. It does seem like a curse. But how?"

Joanna looked at the side of my head. She said, "Your head is totally healed up. I thought your wound looked unexpectedly better yesterday. Maybe *curse* isn't the right word after all."

I said, "I know what this means."

Joanna nodded and said, "Yes. Your dead trees were people. Like you."

I scanned the woods ringing the meadow half-expecting, a dozen tree-people to leap out and carry us off.

I staggered to my feet, spread my arms and said, "Gives new meaning to a nature walk, eh?"

Joanna laughed. She said, "Okay nature boy, but what about shoes?"

I laughed. Then said, "Well. When I was a child, I often hiked barefoot, so it'll be revisiting my youth. My feet are fairly callused. I'll survive. Mostly."

Joanna said, "Okay. Be careful."

I said, "I will. My question for you would be – are you okay? You only slept for couple hours. You mostly just sat there watching me."

Joanna said, "Yeah. I'll be alright. Wait. How do you know that? You could see?"

I said, "Yes. Sort of. I had this weird, immersive and overwhelming perception of everything around me. I could perceive right through and inside things in this bizarre psychedelic layered color scheme or something. Even when I tried to focus on something everything was a swirl of perceptual images."

Joanna said, "That's crazy."

I said, "I know, right?"

I pulled on my jacket and vest. I noticed my phone.

I said, "Did you take any photos?"

Joanna sagged and sighed. She said, "I did. But everything came out totally blurry."

I said, "Like mine, huh?"

Joanna said, "Yeppers."

I said, "Dammit. The tree form must be producing electromagnetic interference or something."

Joanna laughed and said, "Sure. Something."

Walking barefoot in the woods really isn't that bad. The key is using a walking style that keeps all the weight on the back foot while placing the forward foot. If the forward foot senses something pointy or slippery, the back foot maintains balance and weight until the forward foot finds a better spot. Then the walker slowly shifts the weight to the forward foot, ready to lean back if something hurtful that went initially undetected shows up. With practice and experience, a reasonable pace is easy to maintain. Heavy calluses and a high tolerance for pain help, too. However, pine straw with the minor exception of pinecones and well-worn animal paths make for a quicker and easier pace when available.

I felt surprisingly vigorous despite my ordeal. Joanna seemed to be doing reasonably well despite bivouacking on a stone slab.

At one point, I asked, "Are you doing okay?"

Joanna said, "Sure. I'm loving it. We should do this more often."

I said, "Really?"

Joanna said, "Yeah. You know me. I love discomfort."

I said, "Or not."

Joanna laughed. She said, "That is why you like hiking, right? Surviving when things go wrong? A comfortable hike where everything is smooth and easy is like a boring wedding or vacation where nothing goes wrong."

I said, "There is still joy in the experience even if there is no horror story to tell."

Joanna said, "Sure. Sure."

Este Eto

The march back to the cabin was uneventful. But when we emerged from the woods, I was surprised to see Bonnie sitting cross-legged on top of the picnic table. When she saw us, she raised a hand and then covered her mouth. That seemed really odd until I remembered that I was hiking mostly au naturel and we had agreed she would join us for coffee this morning. Instead of covering myself, I waved and kept marching toward the cabin.

I said, "Good morning. Give us about fifteen minutes and we'll be ready to receive guests."

Joanna helpfully said, "There was a clothing accident."

Bonnie nodded with a smirk. She said, "Please take your time and get cleaned up. I arrived early."

I said, "You can come inside."

Bonnie said, "No thank you. I'll just meditate some more until you're ready for me."

I opened the door and followed Joanna inside.

Thirty minutes later, both Joanna and I were clean and wearing sandals, shorts and a tee for me, a tank for her. Bonnie was still sitting where we had left her. She was dressed the same as yesterday except the polo was red instead of blue.

When we approached, Bonnie rolled to her

right and did a vaulting dismount off the picnic table. She looked around with her arms akimbo. She said conspiratorially, “Is the coffee ready? We need to talk. While the day is beautiful, I suspect we would be more comfortable inside as this may take some time.”

I said, “Talk about what?”

Bonnie met my eyes for a long moment and said, “Your situation.”

I said, “What do you know?”

Bonnie shrugged. She said, “I know many things. Some of them are even true.”

Joanna exchanged a confused glance with me. She turned back to Bonnie, “How would you know anything about Garth?”

Bonnie nodded. She said, “Fair question. The important thing is that I know what happened last night in the Grove of the Moon.”

Grove of the Moon?

Joanna looked at me. I shrugged. I said, “Okay. Let’s talk inside.”

Once inside, I motioned for us to sit in the comfortable wooden armchairs that were arrayed around the wooden kitchen table near the fireplace. I had made coffee while Joanna had showered, so I poured a cup for each of us.

I leaned forward and said, “Okay, Bonnie. What do you know and how do you know it?”

Bonnie smiled. She glanced at Joanna and said to me, “Did you transform into something resembling a tree last night.”

Joanna and I gasped. Joanna said, “Were you

there?"

Bonnie said, "No. But the *Omet Eton* destroys anything the person is wearing. Garth had a clothing accident. Given what I know about such things, it is an easy guess."

Joanna said, "You know what this curse is?"

Bonnie said, "Intimately familiar."

Joanna said, "You were there when Garth was injured?"

Bonnie said, "Yes. I am one of the *Este Eto* that were there."

I said, "What?"

Bonnie said, "Tree People. *Este Eto* is Muscogee for Tree People. There were twelve of us there including myself. Our term for transforming into the tree form is *Omet Eton*. It literally means being a tree. Generally speaking, we take precautions to avoid passing the curse onto others, and we had cleared the area before allowing the *Omet Eton*. But we hadn't counted on a nocturnal hiker making an appearance and attempting to hack a limb off Andrew."

Horrified, I spread my hands and said, "Omigawd. I'm so sorry. I enjoy nocturnal hiking. The unexpected appearance took me off-guard. I just wanted a small sample of something I'd never seen before. Again. I'm very sorry."

Bonnie said, "No apology needed. Andrew is fine. He feels terrible himself about infecting you. He slapped the knife out of your hand. The blast to the head was accidental. We don't practice martial tree arts very often."

I said, "Infection? This curse is an infection? A virus? How was I infected?"

Bonnie shrugged and grinned awkwardly. She said, "We're not sure. Our current theory is a magical microbe that is transmittable by bodily fluids."

Joanna said, "Magical?"

Bonnie said, "Microbes don't ordinarily create intricate tattoos that when exposed to moonlight transform the person attached to the tattoo into a tree-thing. And then transform them back when exposed to sunlight."

Joanna said, "Point taken."

I said, "Omigawd. I managed to cut the twig before he whacked me. Then I put my fingers to the head injury. I bet I accidentally transferred fresh sap onto my head injury. If the sap contains the theorized microbe, then that would be a pathway to infection. I definitely had sap on my fingers."

Bonnie said, "Ah. We've never had a definite transmission via sap. Pretty unusual chain of events. Congratulations. You've become part of *Este Eto* lore."

I said, "Should I feel like a winner?"

Bonnie shrugged and said, "It is a curse and a boon."

Joanna interrupted my next question by saying, "How does transmission normally occur?"

Bonnie said, "Like I said. Bodily fluids – just blood or sexual fluids. We don't think it's present in saliva. We believe sexual intercourse has been the most common method."

Joanna gasped and put her hand to her mouth.

I did the same.

Bonnie looked at us carefully. Then she said, "I'm guessing you've had sexual intercourse since the full moon without a condom?"

I said, "We're not married, but we've been exclusive lovers for a long time. Joanna uses birth control."

Bonnie said, "I wasn't judging. But it is likely Joanna is exposed. The tattoo takes one to several days to form, but not everyone exposed becomes an *Este Eto*. Nothing so far?"

I reeled. If Joanna was infected, it was my fault. I couldn't believe this was happening. People didn't turn into trees because of some magical virus or microbe. That was insane. I had gone psychotic. I had to be hallucinating.

Joanna opened her mouth but didn't say anything. She looked down at herself. She said, "Not that I noticed. But I wasn't looking either. The cabin just has a small bathroom mirror."

I said to Bonnie, "Mine is on my back. Where is yours?"

Bonnie laughed hollowly. She said, "It started below my left breast. It quickly spread across my abdomen and down my thighs. And after a while my entire lower body was enveloped. Then it seemed content just to become more intricate and add details, but in recent years it spread up my back across my chest and up over my shoulders."

Bonnie pulled up her right sleeve revealing

intricate green, black and purple lines.

I said, "It grows?"

Bonnie said, "Yes. The tattoos seem to extend with each *Omet Eton.* But the correlation is not exact. The only parts of me unaffected are the ones you can see – my arms, neck and face. It can be rather inconvenient."

I said, "Why?"

Bonnie said, "The tattoos have extended onto the neck, hands and faces of some *Este Eto.* While generally beautiful, facial tattoos are not common and make nightlife for the bearer nearly impossible given the difficulty in blocking the moonlight. I may reach that point soon actually."

Joanna said, "Fuck. Transforming into a tree in the wrong spot could be awkward."

I said, "Tell me about it. I wrecked my bedroom."

Joanna scowled and said, "Wait. What? The nausea you had the other night. Why didn't you say what happened? *Why did you lie to me?*"

Bonnie raised an eyebrow while I squirmed.

I said, "Baby. I was going to bring that up, but at the time, I didn't know what had happened. I thought I had hallucinated. I didn't realize I had transformed into a tree until this morning. And if you remember, I was a bit stressed this morning and didn't think to mention it."

Joanna gave me a crinkled eye look of uncertainty.

Bonnie helpfully said, "The initial *Omet Eton* is always disorienting."

Joanna finally nodded and said, "Okay. But we can't have secrets at a time like this."

Bonnie said, "Well. You're going to want to keep this a secret. Trust me."

With gritted teeth, Joanna said, "From each other."

I said, "Yes, Baby."

Joanna said, "Anyway. What is required to properly block the moonlight? It seemed like Garth's hiking jacket and shirt was enough. Was it?"

Bonnie bobbled her head and said, "Heavy clothing is usually sufficient. Fortunately, the exposure needs to be relatively direct for a period of time modified by the amount of moonlight and exposed tattoo. But once it activates, the *Omet Eton* is unstoppable. All *Este Eto* take precautions against the Moon."

Joanna scowled. She said, "Moonlight is just reflected sunlight. Why doesn't sunlight activate the tattoo?"

Bonnie stared at Joanna for a bit and then frowned. She said, "I don't know. I don't know why moonlight activates the tattoo. Moonlight seems different than sunlight. No?"

Joanna frowned. She said, "Hm. I wonder if simulated moonlight would activate the tattoo. Ever had an unexpected *Omet Eton*?"

Bonnie spread her hands and said, "I'm not sure. Never happened to me. I don't know about the others."

While Joanna's questions seemed relevant and

probably important, I was still freaked out and worried about Joanna being infected. My mind raced with questions of my own. I lost track of the conversation. But then something caught my attention.

I said, "What? How many *Este Eto* are there?"

Bonnie and Joanna stopped talking and stared at me.

Joanna said, "She said there are forty-two counting you."

I said, "That doesn't seem like too many if it can be spread so easily."

Bonnie said, "Once we realized it was sexually transmitted, we've been very careful not to infect others. We've also been very isolated up here."

Joanna said, "So all *Este Eto* live nearby?"

Bonnie smiled. She said, "Until recently, yes. They are only twelve of us currently ensconced up here. We voted to allow the members to explore the world as long as they remained anonymous and prevented transmission."

I said, "Voted?"

Bonnie nodded. She said, "It is complicated. We are a special clan that must maintain a dark secret. Long ago we made oaths that bound us together under our clan rules for the protection of all. Important decisions including where we live have to be approved by the clan. It can be annoying, but it is necessary. With modern communication and the Internet, we decided we could disperse. The world is complex, and we had stayed isolated too long."

I said, "How long has the *Este Eto* clan existed?"

Bonnie looked at me carefully and licked her lips in hesitation. I hated when I asked an unexpectedly awkward question. I was that guy that would invariably ask someone about how their child was doing in school that everyone else knew had been killed in a tragic accident a month ago. Or naively ask the overweight but not pregnant woman when the baby was due. Admittedly, it was a notable ability that served me well when looking for criminal transactions at my job.

Bonnie breathed heavily while Joanna and I waited.

Finally, Bonnie said, "The *Este Eto* have existed for over eight centuries."

I said, "Wow. Has the clan always called this area home?"

Bonnie said, "We spent most of those centuries in hiding. But mostly."

Joanna said, "Why in hiding?"

Bonnie smiled and said, "Modern societies generally leave people to themselves even if it would be better for us to be more neighborly. In the past, most peoples including ours were much more communal and kept careful and close track of everyone nearby even if we respected their privacy. If our secret had been uncovered, we would have been accused of dark sorcery and murdered. We had to stay hidden or risk discovery and horror."

Joanna seemed puzzled by something. She

asked, "How old are you?"

Bonnie hesitated. Then she sighed and bobbled her head. She said, "I'm not sure exactly. It is easy to lose track when it doesn't matter. My best guess is that I was born just before the vernal equinox in eleven seventy plus or minus ten years. So I'm about 850 years old."

Joanna just stared. I couldn't decide what I had heard. I said, "What do you mean?"

Bonnie laughed. She said, "I've lived more than eight centuries."

I stupidly said, "You don't look that old."

Bonnie laughed. She said, "Yes. I'm not nearly as moldy as one would expect."

I said, "I don't see how that's possible."

Joanna snorted. She said, "It seems more plausible than magically transforming into a tree under moonlight."

I said, "True."

Joanna said, "Although I'm guessing at this point, they are related features."

Bonnie nodded. She said, "Yes. We think so."

I said, "Are all of you that old?"

Bonnie shook her head. She said, "No. I am the oldest by a century. Only four are more than 500 years old. Thirty-one are between 100 and 500 years. Five are less than 100 – none younger than sixty. Not counting you."

Joanna said, "Have there been others?"

Bonnie nodded. She said, "Yes. At the time of the Great Plague, we numbered close to eighty. Only five of us survived."

Joanna said, "Omigawd. Smallpox and measles brought by the Conquistadors."

Bonnie nodded sadly. She said, "We don't seem to age, but we are not immune to disease, poison or injury. If we survive an injury or other harm, we do eventually heal almost perfectly although it can take several transformations."

I said, "Ah. The *Omet Eton* restores you and keeps you young?"

Bonnie nodded. She said, "Seemingly so."

I exchanged a bewildered glance with Joanna. This was all too much really. Self-propagating tattoos. Transformation by moonlight. And unnatural youth. It was insane.

Bonnie pursed her lips. She said, "I'm sorry. We didn't want this to happen to you."

I said, "Now what?"

Bonnie said, "I think you should confirm whether or not Joanna has been infected. I'll step outside."

Joanna said, "No. Stay. I'm not shy about my body."

Bonnie said, "As you wish."

Although my brother's cabin was luxurious, it was still designed with efficiency in mind. It actually had only three rooms: the combo mud and laundry room, the bathroom and the main cabin. The main cabin contained the small but full-service kitchen with a rolling island that could be pushed out of the way when not needed. A kitchen table and six chairs were in front of the fireplace opposite the kitchen area. There was a closet and a set of bunk beds tucked against the bathroom wall. A leather sofabed and a Murphy bed faced each other. The main cabin could sleep six comfortably. I preferred the Murphy bed.

I said truthfully, "There's plenty of room for privacy in the bathroom."

Joanna said, "No I prefer for Bonnie to help verify the tattoo."

With that, Joanna turned her back to us and pulled her tank top off and started to undo her bra, but I stopped her with a weak yelp. A small yellow, green, black and red flower and curled stem decorated her lower back just to the left of her spine. This was terrible.

I said, "Oh no. You are infected."

Bonnie said, "I am afraid so. Good spot though. Easy to hide from the Moon."

Joanna said, "The mirror in the bathroom sucks. Take a picture so I can see."

I pulled out my phone and took a picture that captured just her lower back. Then I took a closeup. I showed them to Joanna who seemed pleased rather than upset.

Joanna said, "I'm not a tattoo person, but I would have thought I would have chosen an abstract geometric design. But this one seems quite beautiful."

I said, "You're taking this well."

Joanna said, "Not really. But like you said, now what?"

We turned to Bonnie.

Bonnie shrugged. She said, "Well. By our

clan rules, you are eligible to join us by taking the *Este Eto* Clan Oath. You would then be under the protection of the clan and we would help you adjust, and also conceal your condition."

I narrowed my eyes. I said, "And if we don't?"

Bonnie shrugged sadly and said, "I would probably help you anyway as best I could. But the others might not."

Joanna said, "We would be in danger?"

Bonnie shook her head. She said, "Not from us. Society would be another matter. The others would just be unwilling to help you because that would subject them to potential exposure given your lack of commitment to the clan."

Bonnie seemed sincere but I wasn't entirely convinced that we would be safe from the others in her clan if we refused to join. She was certainly correct that we were likely in danger from the authorities and society in general.

I said, "Have there been others than didn't join?"

Bonnie stared at me carefully and smiled. She said, "Yes."

Joanna said, "And?"

Bonnie laughed. She said, "And we have no idea what happened to most of them. I know several that died ordinary deaths, but those were long ago. Andrew claims he came across one back in the sixties and talked to her, but the woman vanished the next day and he never saw her again."

I said, "Does that worry you?"

Bonnie said, "Yes and no. Our identities are unknown to anyone else at this point in time. We will have to change identities every twenty to thirty years at a minimum since we all look too young for our age."

I inhaled strongly. I often tracked down and exposed falsified identities. I nearly said that I regularly expose fraudulent identities as part of my job, but I don't want to create unnecessary fear at just that moment. Instead I said, "That is becoming more difficult."

Bonnie nodded. She said, "Yes. Extremely difficult. The *Este Eto* will need to learn the necessary skills."

Joanna looked at me, started to say something, and somehow, I intuited what she was thinking and shook my head. She stopped and sat back in her chair. I didn't want her to reveal my expertise in identity fraud.

Joanna said firmly, "I want to experience the *Omet Eton*. Will there be enough Moonlight tonight?"

Bonnie looked momentarily confused by the sudden change in subject. She said, "Yes. The full moon initiates the *Omet Eton* in seconds regardless of other light. A crescent to half moon can take several minutes and can get drowned out by artificial light. Tonight will still be the waning gibbous rising at twelve-thirty. It'll trigger your *Omet Eton* quickly."

Omet Eton

Bonnie recommended a full-length cloak that could be cast aside when an *Este Eto* is ready for the *Omet Eton*. Although I owned a proper rain poncho, I typically only packed a one-time use super-thin plastic emergency poncho for day hiking. And so I had to admit, we didn't really have anything suitable. Bonnie then volunteered to let us use her spares. She headed back to her house to get them. After Bonnie left, Joanna and I stared at each other for a long time.

Finally, I said, "What should we do?"

Joanna said, "I don't know."

I said, "Are you sure you want to do this *Omet Eton*? Maybe antibiotics or some other treatment could stop the infection if you haven't transformed yet?"

Joanna nodded. She said, "I hadn't thought about that. Why wouldn't it be treatable either way?"

I said, "I don't know. I was just speculating."

Joanna lowered her eyes, licked her lips and looked around without looking at me. This was getting crazier by the minute.

Joanna looked up and said, "They are immortal. Don't you want that?"

I said, "They are not immortal. They can die. Bonnie said so. Many have. They just don't age.

Not the same thing."

Joanna said, "But it seems like a damned good thing. Beautiful tattoos and staying away from the moonlight seem the only downside."

I said, "And living in secret."

Joanna laughed. She said, "We do that already. We are not exactly amazingly social."

I nodded. I said, "Well. True. But we'd have to abandon our families at some point. And we have to pledge to not infect anyone else."

Joanna said, "No we don't."

I narrowed my eyes. I said, "I think it would be wrong to infect others."

Joanna said, "With their consent?"

I said, "Not even then. Bonnie has not told us everything. Why would she?"

Joanna said, "I don't know. Do you really think they would harm us to protect their secret?"

I said, "I'm not sure. She seemed sincere. But she could vanish right now. And we'd know nothing – but they know who we are. They must have built up considerable wealth and resources after so many decades. They could kill us."

Joanna looked uncomfortable. She said, "Should we flee?"

I said, "And go into hiding?"

Joanna said, "Aren't we going to have to anyway?"

I said, "Yes. But we'd have their help if we joined the clan. Like I said. Bonnie hasn't told us everything. I think she would never have told us this much if she was just planning to kill us."

Joanna looked worried. She said, "I don't know. She did seem sincere. But if she's telling the truth – she has centuries of experience and practice to appear sincere. If we both died unexpectedly, the GBI might check things out up here and might be able to make a connection to Bonnie or other members of the clan. So they'll want to bring us into their confidence and maneuver us into some situation where they can make us disappear and no connection to their clan gets made."

I considered that. It was not impossible.

I said, "Possibly. But that would imply we are in no danger right now. I agree we need to be wary until we can really trust them."

We continued thinking out various scenarios but decided we would just have to wait and improvise as things developed. A while later, Bonnie returned with two dark green silk cloaks and presented them with silly fanfare to amuse us.

I said, "These are pretty thin. What about wintertime?"

Bonnie made a face of doom. She said, "You must be extra vigilant to avoid transforming when it is freezing outside. More than one *Este Eto* has frozen to death. Only forty years ago, just up the road, Teresa Otter went outside during a cold spell to get more firewood, accidentally transformed and froze to death."

Joanna did not look happy.

Bonnie bobbled her head. She said, "That is not nearly as bad as fifty years ago when Pete

Beaver absently went to the outhouse in the middle of the night and transformed wrecking the outhouse. When the sun came up, he slumped into the cesspool and drowned."

I said, "That's horrible."

Bonnie shrugged and said, "It is a curse. But enough of that. Do you want me to stay and keep watch or do you wish privacy? I think you would be safe out back."

I said, "No. I think I can keep watch myself."

Bonnie said, "Oh. I thought you were going to transform together."

For a fleeting moment, I thought Bonnie was setting us up for something sinister. I said, "Erm. No. I know what it feels like. I kind of wanted to see the transformation for myself."

Bonnie shrugged. She said, "Makes sense. I made a rash delivery promise to a dear friend and so I really need to work on a pair of moccasins this afternoon. Do you mind if I come over at sunrise tomorrow to make sure Joanna is okay?"

I said, "Is there something to be worried about?"

Joanna looked more unhappy.

Bonnie said, "Not really. But I was planning on bringing my supply of medicinals to combat the nausea and confusion if its unexpectedly strong. It does happen. The disorientation and sickness are not directly life threatening – but it can be really uncomfortable sometimes."

Joanna somehow looked even more unhappy.

I said, "Joanna? I think we should have Bonnie

here when you transform back."

Joanna looked to be in pain. She frowned and said, "Yes. That seems like a good idea actually."

Joanna turned to Bonnie. "If you were serious, I would like you to stay over night and help keep watch. While I trust Garth, I'd feel better if you were here as well."

Joanna looked at me for approval. I nodded.

Bonnie smiled beautifully and said, "Of course I was serious. I would be glad to keep watch. By the way, I recommend a nap. And avoid eating or drinking anything except water for several hours before you plan to transform. It seems to help with the nausea from the *Omet Eton*. I'll come down after dinner and my own nap around nine or so."

I walked Bonnie out the door and watched her walk up the road. I returned to sit with a very contemplative Joanna.

I said, "Are you okay?"

Joanna quirked an eyebrow and said, "Yes. Probably."

I said, "I plan to be up all-night keeping watch and you didn't get much rest last night. I suggest we eat lunch and get some sleep."

Joanna nodded and said, "Agreed. I'm running on pure adrenalin."

Several hours later, we woke less sleep deprived but no less apprehensive. I made breakfast for dinner around six. We passed time waiting for Bonnie to come over by watching a harmless movie from my brother's limited cabin collection.

I would have preferred to watch the Braves game – but my brother didn't bother paying for cable and I didn't have an Internet-based subscription plan since I didn't travel much. Privation comes in many forms.

The trivialities of living rarely seem to allow for proper perspective in the moment. But then sometimes I remember that a significant fraction of the modern economy and maybe even human progress is based on either avoiding or improving those trivialities. Yet, each improvement seems to yield additional complexity and mystery that often drives a desire for the simple life. I think that is why I like taking walks in the woods. Or at least I had hoped so. Instead, I had managed to complicate my life immeasurably.

When Bonnie arrived, we talked about leathermaking and moccasins for a while. I decided to probe Bonnie on something that bothered me.

I said, "I hope you don't mind me asking and I hope you understand my curiosity, but I'm surprised your clan hasn't bought a private estate or something more secluded and anonymous. I would imagine that you should have accumulated considerable wealth over just the last century alone."

Bonnie laughed hollowly. She said, "Well. Until very recently, accumulating wealth wasn't really a luxury we had. We had to give up living in our ancestral towns because we were too scared to live amongst ordinary people and instead lived in the deep woods of the mountains here and there. We knew almost every nook of North Georgia. We had limited trade goods – mostly leather goods we made from deerskin like gloves, moccasins and jackets. You have to understand. We were used to living primitively. We just kept doing what we knew. The curse makes us sterile so there are no children. It was like we were frozen in time. To be honest, we were relatively happy and content in our isolation."

Sterile?

I frowned at Joanna. She shrugged in resignation.

Bonnie shook her head. She said, "But then in the 1830s, the Cherokee who had taken over North Georgia and the remaining Muscogee tribes in Alabama were forcibly relocated to Oklahoma in the aftermath of the Red Stick War and the discovery of gold. We withdrew and scattered into the Smoky Mountains. The miners and settlers took the lands. Still, the forested mountains were left wild and we lived much as we had before. We couldn't trade with the white peoples for fear of being exiled or killed, but the remnants of Cherokee in North Carolina proved to be useful trading partners. And anything we couldn't get by trading we acquired by stealth from the people that had stolen our lands."

Not having anything else useful to say, I said, "I'm sorry."

Bonnie shrugged. She said, "The weight of history is borne by us all. Anyway. Things managed to get worse in the 1880s."

Joanna said, "How?"

Bonnie chuckled. She said, "The industrial timber and mining companies showed up. It was horrible. Within a few decades along with the chestnut blight, everything was destroyed. We often ended up living in abandoned homesteads and mining camps. It was a terrible time. The beautiful forest I had lived in for over seven hundred years was ruined and will never be that good again."

I looked out the window into the darkness and imagined industrial ruin.

Bonnie sighed and continued, "In the midst of all that, we decided to figure out the modern world. In 1925, after a great debate, the *Este Eto* undertook a project we called the Great Learning. Although we knew English and Spanish well enough for trading, we naturally preferred Muscogee and couldn't read or write English with any proficiency. Well, except for Andrew. His father was a literate white man and had taught Andrew the basics. Anyway, we spent years learning how to read and write English properly. And be more fluent in spoken English. It was very hard since we had to teach ourselves since we didn't trust anyone."

I said, "Wow. That must have been very hard."

Bonnie tilted her head. She said, "It was hard. But ultimately, it was worthwhile. The modern world is rather amazing. While I mourn the loss of our old world, it's never coming back. The world of my youth. The world before the Europeans came. It's gone. There are definitely some things I don't miss. I don't miss the violence and war. I don't miss rampant disease and infection. I don't miss going hungry."

Joanna and I just nodded.

Bonnie said, "In other words, we are still quite a ways from creating a private estate. One of the reasons we have dispersed is to acquire modern skills and maybe some wealth. Hopefully, it will bring us together instead of tearing the *Este Eto* apart. I have lived a very long time with many sorrows. The future will yield more."

I said, "Sorrows would seem inevitable."

Bonnie said, "Yes. But I don't dwell on the sorrows. I prefer the joys of living.

I said, "I wouldn't argue with that."

Joanna said, "May I change the subject?"

Changing the subject was one of Joanna's best social skills. She had extricated me from numerous awkward social situations that I had created by making a brilliant and confusing tactical or strategic change of subject.

I said, "Please."

Joanna said, "Do clouds affect the moonlight? I mean does it affect the transformation?"

Bonnie looked up at the ceiling as though she could see into the sky. She shrugged and said, "Heavy cloud cover that blocks the moonlight is usually sufficient to prevent transformation, yes. The forecast is hazy but clear for tonight. Shouldn't be a problem. I would never count on cloud cover for proof against transformation. The moonlight diffused through the clouds can still effect transformation, much like the crescent moon."

Joanna and I nodded. I checked my phone. The moonrise was due in thirty minutes.

I said, "Is it best to wait for the moon to be fully risen?"

Bonnie said, "No. Generally, we pick our spot, disrobe and position ourselves about ten minutes before the moonrise. Less chance of ruining clothing or being poorly positioned."

Joanna said, "That makes sense. Let us be about picking a good spot."

Joanna got up, pulled off her clothes and donned the robe.

Joanna said, "Ready."

Bonnie nodded. She turned towards me and said, "I was going to let it be a surprise, but one of the reasons we transform together in the Grove of the Moon is that during the *Omet Eton* we can share feelings and thoughts. It is a very spiritual experience in the right circumstances. I highly recommend the experience. I understand you are reluctant, possibly because you would feel vulnerable. I was telling the truth earlier when I said I will not harm you. I only want to help and protect you. I may not look it, but I am usually just a wise old woman. But you must understand that I have centuries of practice in the arts of hunting, combat and killing. And I'm not squeamish. If I had wanted you dead, you would be dead. But I damned sure don't kill without a good reason."

I frowned. I looked at Joanna who gave a wry smile. I looked back at Bonnie wondering in which way I was being foolish. I decided she was right. And I decided to foolishly trust her.

I turned to Joanna and said, "Do you wish me to join you?"

Joanna nodded. She said, "Apparently I have an adventurous streak I did not know I had. Please join me."

Joanna smiled at Bonnie who returned the smile. Bonnie said, "I will go with Joanna outside so you can change into your robe with some privacy."

I nodded in appreciation and ignored the fact I would be disrobing in front of Bonnie anyway for the *Omet Eton* and had already seen me half-naked. I needed Joanna to change the subject again.

Outside, Bonnie helped us find level spots far enough apart to avoid tangling branches. And then we faced each other, bowed slightly and disrobed. We positioned ourselves so that our backs would be to the moonrise. Bonnie stood watching arms akimbo with her gaze mostly focused on the horizon. I tried to just float waiting for the moonrise. I stole an occasional glance at Joanna, but she seemed perfectly relaxed and still – probably utilizing her extensive yoga training.

Unlike the previous two events, the transformation was not so abrupt this time. I felt the tattoo warm on my back. I felt my limbs slowly start to stiffen. I was able to bring my feet together and extend my arms as Bonnie had instructed. Everything fuzzed to gray then black. The blackness seemed to last longer than usual. *Or not.*

The psychedelic feeling experience soon followed. I could sense Bonnie, the cabin, my vehicle, and Joanna. Or rather Joanna - the tree edition. I focused on Joanna looking for the special connection Bonnie mentioned. Instead I was flooded with a sensation of overwhelming joy that was not my own. I reeled unable to control the feelings that flowed through and over me.

I thought, "Joanna?"

Nothing. Just more feelings of joy mixed with bewilderment. *Or not.*

I focused my attention on Joanna. I could sense her form, but it was much fuzzier than everything else. I tried to focus more strongly on her branches but that seemed to make the fuzz even worse. I tried to relax my focus, but she just smeared into the background. I was very disappointed to say the least.

"Open your mind and let me speak to you."

That seemed to be a non sequitur. By definition, if I could hear that, I was already open to be spoken to. *Or not.*

I thought, "I'm here. I'm listening."

"Please open your mind. Don't be closed."

I thought, "Can you hear me?"

"Yes. But I want to feel your thoughts. Relax and be open."

The flood of joy changed to a storm of indecision and mild frustration or maybe concern. *But was I that closed? My core feelings were what?* I tried to float which I hoped would open my mind in the way she wanted.

"You seem lost and diffuse or something."

I decided that floating wasn't helping. And it seemed hard to relax when your body was by definition in tension. Focusing on Joanna hadn't helped. I attempted to wave my limbs in frustration.

"Wow. I sense unhappiness. Are you okay?"

I thought, "I am now. Give me a moment."

In the most cliché way possible, I tried to recall happy thoughts of traipsing through the moonlit woods as a young child. I tried to step into those memories and find the joy. It was in that moment that I first understood that my nocturnal adventures had never given me a joyful experience like food or entertainment or sex. Instead, I was always chasing a weird admixture of danger and wonder.

While wonder can create joy in the right circumstance, my intentions were simultaneously wild and clinical. It was like I was trying to find my animal spirits not with smoke to induce mild hypoxia or an intoxicant to produce euphoria, but instead with a boring blend of balanced diet and regular exercise. Coolly stalking my way through the woods was too much like a jungle cat prowling around. Why had I devoted so much energy to something that didn't actually give me joy? My branches drooped forlornly. *Or not.*

"I am sorry Garth. I didn't realize how depressed you were."

I thought, "What? I'm not depressed."

"That is not what I am feeling."

I attempted to will myself into feelings of joy which worked about as well as might be expected. I sighed. *Or not.* Being unable to breathe or move ordinarily made the physics of emotional reactions and body language complicated to the realm of pointless. I shook with frustration. *Or not.*

"Wow. Are you mad at me?"

I thought, "What? Gawd no. I'm sorry. I've screwed everything up. I've ruined your experience."

"Never mind that. I should have been more sensitive to your feelings."

I thought, "I'm just suffering from the stress and disorder of the last several days. You seem to be handling the chaos better than me."

A weird echoing feeling of laughter washed over me. Then something like a wistful sigh.

"You know how our jobs are very similar, but our approach is completely different?"

I thought, "I guess so."

"Sure it is. My entire work-life is centered around putting numeric values that comprise the complete picture onto the scattered chaos of corporate activity where the denizens are either deliberately or incompetently obscuring reality. You seemingly focus on just finding the discordant in the background noise. For you, the big picture is just a convenient filter to

amplify the hidden patterns. I'm foolishly trying to make sense of the big picture. I think you just bask in its wonder."

Joanna was not normally that philosophical. She was always Captain Practical. Suddenly, it made my relationship with wonder and joy make a lot more sense.

I thought, "I never thought about it that way. But I think you are right."

I decided the stress and shock of the *Omet Eton* had suppressed my natural wonder. I decided to settle into my natural state of observational wonder without floating.

"Wow. You are suddenly open. I can feel your wonder. That seems very soothing. I should try that myself more often. I know I'm too much Captain Practical."

I thought, "Only in a good way."

"I love you."

I thought, "I love you more."

"Let us be silent and just enjoy the sharing of wonder and joy."

I answered with silent wonder.

Medical Advice

Unlike my two previous transformations that seemed interminable, this one ended almost without warning because I was still lost in the *wonder*. Unfortunately, the nausea and vertigo were just as overwhelming as the previous times. I was worried about Joanna, but it is hard to focus when you are dry heaving. She appeared at my side unexpectedly. I took that as a good sign that she was less affected than me.

Joanna said, "Are you alright, Love?"

I said, "Sure. I'm good."

Or not. I hacked up some phlegm and shivered from the wracking nausea.

She handed me my borrowed cloak. I pulled it on with some difficulty. And then squatted with my arms dangling.

Joanna said, "That was amazing."

I nodded in agreement trying not to choke.

Bonnie appeared and said, "Did you vomit the previous times?"

I nodded.

Bonnie said, "Okay. Good. Nothing new. Here drink this. It'll help."

Bonnie handed me a small glass of a brownish liquid. I gave it a taste. It was sweet and tingling. In my extremity, I had lost my natural paranoia and I just sucked it down. Whether it was just placebo effect or real, my nausea cleared almost immediately.

I sighed deeply in relief and stood up.

I said, "Wow. Thanks. I feel much better already."

Bonnie nodded. She said, "It is ginger root extract mixed with cypress oil, honey and soda water. It usually works quickly."

I said, "I could use some coffee."

Bonnie smiled and said, "Already made. Come."

A few minutes later sipping my coffee, I said, "What now?"

Bonnie said, "You need to make some decisions. Specifically, do you wish to join the *Este Eto* Clan?"

I said, "What is the process?"

Bonnie said, "Nothing complicated. I represent you to the members. We vote. If a two-thirds majority vote approval, you are accepted, and you then take the oath before an assembly of the members."

I said, "What happens if we aren't approved?"

Bonnie said, "Well. Technically, since we formally wrote up the *Este Eto* Clan rules back in the forties, we haven't actually had an applicant since members have either followed the rules properly or haven't admitted to an accidental transmission like what happened to you. According to the rules, you simply won't gain the protection of the *Este Eto* and access to our secrets such as they are."

Joanna said, "But you already told us many secrets."

Bonnie said, "I wasn't supposed to."

Worried, I said, "Will you be in trouble?"

Bonnie shrugged and said, "Only if you refuse to join the *Este Eto* Clan and then reveal what you know."

Joanna said, "What about us?"

Bonnie shrugged again and said, "Unless you take the oath, we won't take action against you. But we won't help you either when the authorities whisk you away someplace 'safe'."

I said, "Has that happened?"

Bonnie gritted her teeth and said, "I have told you everything I can at this point. Why don't you take some time to think about it? I will give you my phone number and you can just text or call me when you decide."

I nodded and considered.

Joanna said, "Why are you so resistant Garth?"

I looked back and forth between Joanna and Bonnie. Joanna looked unhappy while Bonnie remained placid. I still wasn't convinced I should trust Bonnie or the *Este Eto*.

I said, "I need some time to think. I want to return home and give proper consideration."

Bonnie nodded. The Joanna Happiness Index continued to trend downward.

Citing needs of sleep and chores to be done, Bonnie bid us goodbye after extracting a promise of giving her our decision by tomorrow evening. We packed up and headed to Joanna's place.

Although the argument continued during the drive, Joanna was her almost annoyingly level-headed, practical self, and allowed me time to brood over the matter.

Eventually I made a decision as we neared Joanna's place in Roswell.

I said, "Before I agree to join the *Este Eto,* I want to consult Doctor J."

Joanna nodded. She said, "I understand. But I don't like it. What if Bonnie is right about the authorities whisking you away?"

I said, "I won't tell her about Bonnie or you. But I've got to get her advice."

Joanna said, "No. You should tell her about me. Doctor J should know it is sexually transmittable."

I said, "That increases the danger."

Joanna said, "Yes. But if you really want medical advice, don't you need to give the advisor the full story?"

I said, "But that would mean I need to tell her about the *Este Eto* Clan, right?"

Joanna said, "Probably. That could mean ruin, though."

I said, "Dammit. Okay. I don't want to bring ruin to the *Este Eto*. I'll just risk giving the incomplete story."

The Joanna Happiness Index continued to spiral downward, however.

The worried medical assistant worked me into the schedule when I called and said that my symptoms had worsened. We dropped off our stuff at Joanna's house and headed over to the doctor's office that happened to be close by. The waiting room just had a couple of folks who smiled warmly at us. Doctor J ran an efficient practice and the spacious waiting room was rarely full except during flu season. We checked in and were called back after just a short wait.

Doctor J arrived after a five-minute wait in the exam room. I introduced Joanna as my girlfriend.

Doctor J said, "Okay. What's going on?"

I glanced briefly at Joanna who squeezed my hand in encouragement. I said, "Something crazy has happened to me. And I believe my encounter with the tree the other night is the cause."

Doctor J said, "Crazy? Like what?"

I said, "Like I now have a large pseudo-tattoo on my back that I think was caused by a microbe."

Doctor J said, "What? You got a tattoo?"

I said, "I didn't get one. It just appeared overnight while I was sleeping and I'm sure it caused my nausea episode. Like I said, I think its an infection."

Doctor J shook her head and folded her arms. She said, "What? Let me see this thing."

I pulled my shirt off and turned to show her the pseudo-tattoo.

Doctor J, while puling on gloves, said, "That is amazingly intricate."

Doctor J touched the pseudo-tattoo and prodded around a bit.

Doctor J asked, "Does that cause discomfort or pain? Has it been tender? Is it itchy?"

I said, "No pain. No soreness. Not itchy today.

Slightly before."

Doctor J asked, "Why do you think it is an infection?"

I said, "What else would create a pattern like that over night? I didn't suffer a back injury as best I could tell. It doesn't hurt. And Joanna has been seemingly infected as well. She has a different looking pseudo-tattoo that developed yesterday."

Doctor J looked at Joanna in alarm. "Show me."

Joanna dutifully removed the pullover blouse and turned for Doctor J.

Doctor J stepped back and said, "No pain? Soreness? Do you feel okay? Nausea like Garth?"

Joanna shook her head, "No Doctor. I feel completely fine."

Doctor J opened a cabinet and pulled out a digital skin camera microscope and plugged it in. She said, "This is the latest device for examining skin for cancer and other problems."

Doctor J peered for several minutes at the pseudo-tattoos on first me and then Joanna. She stepped back and put the instrument down. Then she pulled off the gloves and went over to the computer station where she typed and scrolled around a bit. She rubbed her jaw. Then typed some more. Scrolled and clicked. Scrolled and clicked. More typing. Finally a big sigh.

Worried, I said, "What is it, doctor?"

Doctor J looked at me, frowned and said, "I have no idea. To me, it actually looks like a professionally done tattoo. And the computer medical diagnostic tools are completely convinced it is a standard, permanent tattoo with pigmentation embedded in the dermis – but with unusual and unidentified pigments. You aren't just messing with me, are you?"

Puzzled, I shook my head. I said, "Getting a permanent tattoo just to play a joke on my doctor? And convincing my girlfriend to play along as well?"

Joanna said, "I don't do jokes."

Doctor J nodded. She said, "Okay. Probably not. What other symptoms have you had?"

I said, "Besides the nausea, nothing else noticeable."

Joanna bit her lip. She said, "Garth is lying. When the tattoos are exposed to moonlight, we temporarily transform into tree-things."

Doctor J stared. Then blinked and shook her head. She said, "What did you say?"

I said, "She said that we transform into trees when the infected skin is exposed to enough moonlight. And then change back into people when the sun rises."

Doctor J lowered her head and stared. She said, "You mean like a werewolf?"

I said, "Yeah. Sort of like that, I guess. Except we can't actually move around being trees and not being particularly bloodthirsty or anything. It's a weird psychedelic experience to be honest."

Joanna said, "I saw it happen to him. And then I experienced the transformation myself after my infection developed into a tattoo."

Doctor J said, "So. Let me get this straight. You believe you've gotten some kind of infection that created a tattoo that when exposed to moonlight transforms you into a tree?"

Joanna and I looked at each other and nodded.

Doctor J asked, "How is the infection transmitted?"

Joanna said confidently, "We're pretty sure by bodily fluids. At least, that is how I got it from Garth."

Doctor J nodded and breathed heavily. "And how did Garth get infected?"

I said, "My encounter with the tree."

Doctor J looked at me thoughtfully. She said, "So was this tree was a weretree?"

I said, "I don't know. It wasn't there when I returned to look for it the next day."

Doctor J said, "Oh."

Joanna said, "Exactly."

In perfect neutral doctor tone, Doctor J said, "You can put your shirts back on."

Doctor J grabbed her own shoulders in thought and some obvious distress. She breathed heavily. We waited while Doctor J continued to consider.

Finally, I said, "Doctor?"

Doctor J shook her head. She said, "Your bloodwork didn't show anything unusual that would indicate an obvious immune reaction. That is not conclusive though. I want to consult with a specialist, Doctor Thor Anderson. He is a close friend of mine. He works for the CDC. Would that be okay?"

I looked at Joanna. She shrugged. This could quickly get out-of-hand. Bonnie's warning about being whisked away gave me terrible pause. My paranoias were suddenly overlapping and contradictory.

Recognizing our hesitancy, Doctor J said, "Thor can be trusted. He won't tell anyone else about your condition without your permission. And neither will I."

I looked at Joanna again. The Joanna Happiness Index was not improving, but she nodded assent. I said, "Okay. You can consult with Doctor Anderson. But only him."

Doctor J said, "Of course. I will contact him right now."

Doctor J pulled out her phone and texted something.

Within moments her phone played Enya's *Orinoco Flow*, she answered with a quiet voice, "Hi Thor. Thanks for calling."

A muffled deep male voice answered.

Doctor J said, "Yeah. I have a patient and his girlfriend that I need to talk to you about. And I promised them complete privacy. They are in the room with me in my Roswell office."

Muffled voice. Doctor J waited patiently to silence. More muffled voice.

Doctor J said, "Can I put you on speaker?"

Muffled voice. Doctor J held the phone out and pressed the speaker icon.

Doctor J said, "You're on speaker, Thor. My patients, whose names I won't disclose yet are in the room with me."

Thor said, "Good morning. What is troubling you?"

Doctor J nodded to me.

I said, "Um. Good morning Doctor Anderson--"

Thor said, "Please call me Thor. I prefer to be informal."

I was thrown slightly off balance. I said, "Okay. As you wish. The trouble is what I believe to be a strange infection that has created a pseudo-tattoo-thing on my back that when exposed to moonlight transforms me into a tree-thing. Worse, my girlfriend also is infected, we believe by sexual transmission."

Without the expected pause of surprise, Thor said, "And you transform back into your normal self when the sun rises?"

I said, "Erm. Yes. Obviously, it was only temporary."

Thor said, "Would it be okay I examined you myself?"

I looked around somewhat confused. I said, "Okay."

Doctor J said, "When? Where?"

Thor said, "I'm currently in Chicago. I'm flying back late this evening. How about we all meet at ten tomorrow morning at your office Juliana?"

Doctor J said, "Uh. Checking schedule… Erm. Yes. That's fine with me."

Doctor J looked at us expectantly.

I looked at Joanna once more and she nodded. I said, "Yes. That is okay with us."

Doctor J said, "Okay then. Tomorrow at ten."

Thor said, "Good. See you then."

Doctor J said, "Are there any tests you want me to run before then?"

Thor said, "No."

We nodded. Doctor J said, "Very good then."

Doctor J pressed an icon and put the phone away.

I said, "Thank you Doctor."

Doctor J smiled, opened the door and said, "See y'all tomorrow. And stay out of the moonlight I would think."

I said, "Will do."

Second Thoughts

Joanna watched impatiently over my shoulder as I sat hunched over my work laptop on her kitchen table.

Joanna said, "Can you get into trouble looking up Anderson like that on your work systems?"

I said, "No. I'm allowed and encouraged to do background checks on my personal and professional contacts using our systems and vendors. I'm supposed to make sure those contacts are not security risks that might be trying to leverage their relationship with me to gain information about our systems. I am supposed to report all of my new and continuing contacts periodically. It is kind of annoying actually. Not as bad as your father with his Top Secret clearance crap."

Joanna giggled and said, "He has to go through security clearance checks regularly. He finds the process very intrusive."

I said, "Yeah. Nothing that bad."

Joanna said, "Do you look me up?"

I shrugged and said, "Yes. As you well know, you're squeaky clean."

Joanna harrumphed.

I ignored her and examined the background check results.

I said, "Hey. Doctor Anderson has US Top

Secret and Sensitive Compartmented Information clearance. Hun."

I looked at the available CDC information.

I said, "Woah. He is a formal advisor to the biological warfare response teams. I guess he really is an expert, eh?"

Joanna said, "I hope so. But will he be able to help us? Do we really want his help?"

I said, "I'm not sure."

Joanna looked thoughtful, then puzzled. Then she said, "Now that I think about it. I got the distinct impression Thor was familiar with our condition."

I said, "How could that be?"

Joanna said, "I dunno. But he didn't seem appropriately skeptical. And not really that surprised. I would have been."

I said, "I had that same feeling but I thought I was just caught up in the moment. That doesn't make any sense."

Joanna said, "I guess we add that to the list."

I said, "Yeah."

I spent nearly an hour scanning the background reports, but there was nothing remarkable except that Anderson had an extensive career as an infectious disease researcher, investigator and manager.

Eventually, Joanna sat down opposite me and sighed heavily.

I looked at her expectantly.

Joanna cringed in apparent pain. She said, "What if he can have us whisked away as Bonnie warned?"

I breathed heavily. I said, "Unfortunately, I think he probably can. I'm now worried I have fucked up. I'm sorry. This is all my fault."

Joanna said, "I could have talked you out of it."

I said, "I guess. What do we do now?"

Joanna said, "Maybe we should go into hiding?"

I said, "I think we need to know what he knows before we do something drastic."

Joanna said, "Only if he doesn't have us whisked away."

I said, "True. But going into hiding isn't that easy or comfortable."

Joanna said, "Aren't you an expert in that area?"

I said, "I am an expert at finding hidden money and exposing false identities which is not quite the same as staying hidden from the government. I guess I should start researching that though…"

Joanna said, "It was your idea to seek medical advice."

I said, "I said I was sorry."

Joanna sighed. She said, "I know. I know. He works for the CDC. I would think he takes medical ethics pretty seriously. And Doctor J seems to believe he would maintain our privacy which I think would rule out whisking us away."

I said, "Not if he believes we are a serious public safety risk."

Joanna said, "Are we?"

I said, "What would he do if we were werewolves?"

Joanna said, "I dunno. I think he would try to cure us."

I said, "Probably. But first he would quarantine us in a secure facility for everyone's protection."

Joanna sighed. She said, "Maybe he would make it seem rational rather than just using force."

I said, "Probably. But if I were him, I would have a backup plan that involved more persuasive means."

I pressed my hands against my forehead. There are many ways to fuck up your life. One of them is worrying too much about things that won't actually happen. Another is failing to worry about things that might happen. Yet another is being paralyzed by trying to decide which is which.

Joanna said, "I think we decide in the morning. But I want to talk about something else."

Grateful for a tactical change of subject, I closed the laptop and said, "Good."

Joanna said, "What did you think of last night?"

I said, "Well. Trying to connect with you did not go too well. I wonder how the *Este Eto* experience it."

Joanna said, "I think we struggled at first, but then it was good once we worked through things."

I said, "I dunno. Bonnie seemed to think it was supposed to be a spiritual experience. That didn't feel spiritual to me. It just felt more like how we like to sit and watch the sunset sometimes without talking."

Joanna said, "Yeah. I thought that was very us, though."

I said, "Maybe it takes more practice for some. Where some, would be, me."

Joanna said, "Or maybe we don't understand spiritual experiences. And we were actually having one."

I said, "As likely as not knowing us."

Joanna looked around the kitchen and crinkled her face. I watched her with bemusement. I sensed a change of subject coming.

Joanna said, "What are you going to do about your town home?"

I said, "Well. That kind of depends. Are we going to flee into hiding? Are we going to be whisked away temporarily or permanently by the government? I was thinking of just staying here until we figured things out since my bedroom is a mess and I would need to hang blackout curtains to sleep there anyway. That's okay right?"

Joanna bobbled her head. She said, "Of course. I was going to suggest you move your things here. I have plenty of room. I think we can adjust ourselves to living together until things play out."

I said, "Well. Okay. Sure. Makes sense to have a plan for that."

Joanna said, "Good."

I said, "So we aren't going to flee?"

Joanna said, "That would seem premature

especially without adequate planning. And I know you want to learn more about the condition. Maybe the doctor really does know what has happened to us and make you feel more comfortable with the condition."

I said, "Okay. I'll be optimistic."

Joanna said, "If he does make you comfortable, will you agree to join the *Este Eto*?"

I said, "You want that don't you?"

Joanna nodded. She said, "I want to explore what we are. I think you should be less afraid and embrace it."

I nodded. Joanna was probably right. She often was.

The Joanna Happiness Index was trending higher.

Thor

Doctor Thor Anderson arrived in green hospital scrubs and red-black cross-trainers. He was lean, average height, blue eyes, brownish hair with a touch of gray and a craggy face. Doctor J closed the door to her spacious office behind them as they entered. She made introductions and seated everyone in a circle.

Thor said, "Please explain the full circumstances."

I spent twenty minutes explaining my initial nighttime encounter with the tree and subsequent events while leaving out Bonnie and the *Este Eto* entirely. Thor listened patiently and attentively asking no questions. When I was finished, he nodded thoughtfully.

Thor said, "Did Doctor J tell you what I actually do?"

I said, "No. She just said you were a specialist at the CDC. Is that not true?"

Doctor J looked sharply at Thor.

Thor said, "No. That is very true. I am a veteran infectious disease researcher. I'm an informal advisor to various CDC teams including the surveillance division. But that is not my primary function."

Doctor J said, "What?"

Thor nodded sadly and said, "My primary

function is top secret."

Doctor J said, "Figures."

Thor looked around. He said, "Circumstances being what they are. I'll need to explain that function. I must ask you not to reveal anything I am about to say."

Joanna looked nervously at me. Paranoia gripped me, but I said, "And if we do?"

Thor looked grave. He said, "Government agents would whisk all of us away and we would never be heard from again."

The Joanna Happiness Index dived to a new low.

Doctor J said, "What are you talking about Thor? This is no time for jokes."

Thor shrugged. He said, "If only this were a joke. May I have your word of honor not to repeat or reveal anything I'm going to tell you? Otherwise I cannot help you."

I said, "Okay. You have my word. I will reveal nothing."

I looked at Joanna. She nodded and said, "I will also reveal nothing."

We turned to look at Doctor J who looked very nonplussed.

Doctor J said, "I am duty-bound not reveal confidential patient information. I will reveal nothing discussed here under that umbrella."

Thor nodded. He said, "Very good then. We are bound to secrecy."

Thor looked around the room conspiratorially and then continued, "Several years ago when the zombie mania became wildly popular, the White House secretly ordered the CDC to monitor for anything that could create zombies or other supernatural things. The Director of the CDC thought it was patently ridiculous, of course, but the looneys were insistent. To placate them, she asked for a ridiculous budget that was unexpectedly doubled and granted out of some secret DOD fund. And so the Zombie Investigation Team was born. The Director decided I was the perfect person to be in charge of the team."

Doctor J, once again, said, "What?"

Thor nodded with a smirk.

Joanna said, "Why were you the perfect person?"

Thor crooked an eyebrow and said, "Because she knew I would find useful ways to spend the money and generate the right reports to keep the funding going."

I said, "Wouldn't sanity eventually prevail and pull the funding?"

Thor laughed and said, "Well. It's just a few million tucked away in the DOD black ops budget. And my reports are written just the right way to keep the bureaucrats happy that the money is being well spent."

I said, "How big is the team?"

Thor said, "That is a complete secret. Only the Director and the Deputy Director know who is on the team and they keep the case officer happy. The team is just me, a medical records officer and a data scientist – but the DOD is led to believe it's a large and extensive team. Given that there is no actual zombie threat, we allocate the funds to further research in more useful areas. For example, we help fund rabies monitoring which admittedly is a straight up foaming at the mouth zombie horrorshow. So technically, we are really spending some of the money on actual zombie prevention."

Joanna said, "But what does your bureaucratic shenanigans matter to us? We need your expertise in infectious disease. You didn't need to tell us about your secret function."

Thor nodded. He said, "Well. A funny thing happened along the way. As I mentioned, we are also mandated with investigating and monitoring other supernatural things caused by infectious agents. And so the Director occasionally refers the weird stuff to the Zombie Investigation Team."

Thor paused seemingly for dramatic effect.

Thor said, "The trouble is some of the weird stuff turned out to be unexpectedly unusual."

I said, "Like what?"

Thor said, "Like *Este Eto*."

Joanna gasped.

Doctor J said, "What?"

I said, "It's Muscogee for Tree People."

Thor smiled. He said, "I suspected you were leaving something out."

I said, "And what do you know about the *Este Eto*?"

Thor laughed. He said, "Not nearly enough. Three years ago, someone managed to hack into a CDC surveillance record system. The system has the original medical records collected during medical surveillance work and is considered highly confidential and generally well-protected. For patient privacy reasons, those records are then scrubbed of information that would identify the patient and put into a different record system for researchers to use. Because the CDC is involved in NBC response and surveillance, our systems are under the purview of the US Cyber Command."

Doctor J said, "NBC?"

Thor said, "Sorry. Nuclear, biological and chemical terrorism and warfare."

Doctor J said, "Right. I think I knew that."

Thor continued, "Cyber Command personnel tracked the hacker down to a person living in Georgia. The person had used some of the stolen NSA tools and generally had done a good job covering her tracks by routing through VPN servers in Lithuania, but the US Cyber Command claimed they had managed to compromise the particular server she was using. And the interesting part was the particular records she was perusing were flagged for my team. At my request, they initiated a complete surveillance operation including all communications and direct audio and visual capture.

I said, "Her name?"

Thor said, "I wish to keep that secret for now."

I shrugged.

Thor continued, "We discovered that she belonged to this secret society called the *Este Eto* with unusual tattoos and an interest in creating new identities. But she vanished after just a few months and everything we had been monitoring went cold and stale."

I said, "Did she discover she was under watch somehow?"

Thor shrugged. He said, "Most likely."

Joanna said, "I think you said she was looking at records that were flagged for your team. What was special about them?"

Thor's eyes twinkled. He said, "You see. Four years ago, a man with unusual tattoos was found naked and frozen to death on a remote farm in Vermont by the local sheriff after a neighbor reported him missing. The coroner had concluded that hypothermia induced madness had probably caused him to discard his clothes since there were no signs of foul play – but no clothes were ever discovered other than a jacket."

Joanna said, "While obviously tragic, why would that be flagged for your team?"

Thor said, "Well. The Vermont State Police conducted an investigation given the possibility of homicide. They found a diary written by the man that claimed he could turn into a tree. They, of course, assumed that the victim was delusional. But he had no known mental health issues or risk factors. The autopsy tissue and blood samples were referred to the CDC for analysis to determine if he possibly had suffered from an infection or toxin induced delirium and had wandered outside unclothed except for the jacket.

And so the case had gotten referred to me. But toxicology was negative, and it is very difficult to isolate an unknown pathogen from a deceased individual and unsurprisingly we were unable to find anything. It was weird enough though that I flagged it for my team to watch."

I said, "Fuck."

Thor said, "Indeed. Once we learned what we did from the hacker, the Vermont case became even more interesting. And so we investigated further."

Joanna said, "What did you find?"

Thor sighed and said, "Nothing."

I said, "Hun."

Thor said, "But instead someone found us."

Suddenly, my phone started playing the Bangles *Manic Monday* – my default ringtone. I checked the number – it was Bonnie Otter. I hesitated. My distress must have been sufficiently obvious that everyone motioned for me to answer. I had intended to let it drop to voicemail – but instead I swiped to answer and pulled the phone to me ear.

I said, "Hey. This is Garth. Can I call you back in a few minutes?"

Bonnie said, "Is Thor there yet?"

I froze for a long moment…

Finally, I said, "Unh-huh."

Bonnie said, "Good. You can trust him."

I said, "Um…"

Bonnie said, "Let me talk to Thor."

Completely unnerved, I presented the phone

to Thor. I said, "It's Bonnie Otter. She wants to talk to you."

Thor smiled and took the phone. He said, "Hi Bonnie."

Thor grunted a couple of times and finally said, "Okay."

Thor handed the phone back.

Bonnie said, "Listen to Thor."

I said, "Okay."

Thor said, "You really need to agree to join the *Este Eto* at this point. Otherwise government agents will indeed likely whisk us all away."

Joanna said, "Are you a member?"

Thor smiled. He said, "I am not. I'm from Denmark. I don't have the required Muscogee DNA."

I said, "What?"

Thor said, "So far, no one that has been exposed to the *Este Eto Organism* that doesn't have Muscogee DNA has shown any symptoms or other signs of infection. And most Muscogee seem unaffected as well when exposed. You two appear to be unlucky in that respect."

Joanna said, "Hun. My maternal grandmother's father was said to be a member of the Muscogee Nation in Oklahoma. I guess he really was. People tend to make those stories up. I guess to excuse themselves of responsibility or something by being related to the victims."

But I don't have Muscogee DNA. Or not?

Joanna looked at me. She said, "You never mentioned Native American ancestry."

I said, "I wasn't aware I had any."

Everyone shrugged.

I said, "Organism? Have you isolated it? Virus?"

Thor frowned. He said, "Well, we've only been working on the organism for a few months now. Preliminary work hasn't actually produced an identifiable isolate. But we're certain that it is only a matter of time. We're hoping we'll be able to isolate the critical DNA and possibly the infectious organism sooner rather than later. My current theory is that it is a prion."

Doctor J said, "Ignoring that this is completely impossible except that everyone here and on the phone believes that it is true, what is the plan?"

Thor said, "Garth and Joanna join the *Este Eto* clan. My team continues researching this most interesting phenomena with the cooperation of Bonnie and the *Este Eto*. Everyone is protected by the secrecy umbrella of my unit including the ability to create government identities should we need to hide people from the authorities."

I said, "Fake identities?"

Thor shook his head. He said, "No. Real government, valid identities including all the necessary records."

Joanna said, "But aren't you part of the authorities?"

Thor nodded. He said, "Yes. The US security apparatus is rather expansive and not everyone has the same enlightened view of the situation that my team does – where not everyone means virtually everyone."

Joanna said, "Oh. Yes, that makes sense."

I said, "About the only thing that does."

I sighed and looked at Joanna. I said, "Agreed?"

Joanna nodded.

I held the phone up and said, "Okay. Bonnie. You win. Joanna and I agree to join the *Este Eto*."

Bonnie said, "Good. The ceremony is planned for Saturday night and I'll get a vote done this evening. And remember to mind the moonlight."

I said, "Yes. Thank you."

Joanna said, "What about Doctor J?"

Doctor J looking surprised said, "What about me?"

Joanna said, "Doesn't she need protection as well? Someone might come asking being that she is Garth's regular doctor."

Thor cocked his head and said, "Yes. You are correct. No problem. I will hire her as a secret consultant for my team."

Doctor J looked nonplussed. She said, "What do I have to do?"

Thor shrugged. He said, "Anything you want to do to help. Or nothing as you choose. Either way, you can legally refuse any inquiries and refer them to me. And should need arise I can probably provide protection under my team's umbrella. If you do provide help, I will gladly compensate you appropriately."

Doctor J said, "Works for me."

I ended the call and looked at Joanna.

Joanna smiled and said, "I know this might

seem an odd time, but will you marry me?"

I blinked and my mouth fell half open. Then I recovered with a broad smile and said, "You know what. I'm probably suffering from too much stress. But the answer is 'yes'. This is the strangest week of my life. Might as well make it stranger."

Doctor J said, "Aren't you going to kiss?"

Joanna and I both stared at Doctor J.

Thor laughed.

I stood up and said, "Fine then. Joanna?"

Joanna stood up and we embraced and briefly kissed. Paused. And then kissed some more.

Doctor J said, "I know this is an emotional moment – but I've got patients to see. Stay as long as you need, though, the office closes at five."

We waved as she left.

Thor said, "I really need to get down to my office as well. I need to make sure I've got all the necessary protections in place immediately."

We waved as he left.

Joanna kissed me some more and said, "Let's go back to my place for some celebratory Champagne. Besides we've got phone calls to make."

Alarmed, I said, "To whom?"

Joanna looked puzzled. She said, "My family. Your family. Our friends. We're finally getting married. They'll be ecstatic."

Relieved, I said, "Right. Yes. That'll be fun."

Or not.

www.ingramcontent.com/pod-product-compliance
Lightning Source LLC
Chambersburg PA
CBHW030335310726
48979CB00001B/37
* 9 7 8 1 9 4 4 7 1 4 0 5 5 *